6 ½ BODY PARTS

by STEPHANIE BOND

a Body Movers novella

Front cover by Andrew Brown at clicktwicedesign.com
All rights reserved.
ISBN: 0989042960
ISBN 13: 9780989042963

CHAPTER ONE

CARLOTTA WREN JARRED AWAKE, her muscles seized in terror. Disoriented, she gulped air, her chest pumping furiously as her gaze darted around the darkened room.

Nothing… Her bedroom was still and quiet, as was the entire townhouse— peacefully silent at 4:34 AM… just as if everything in the world was okay.

As if.

She closed her eyes until the demons in her dreams retreated to the corners of her mind and her heart rate slowed. The pulse reverberating in her ears sounded bumpy and hesitant, evidence that her heart had taken more than a few hits lately.

She shifted on the warm pillow a millimeter and pain lit up her shoulder, a grim reminder that a madman had had her in his clutches only hours before. She and Peter Ashford had been planning to leave for Las Vegas for some much needed alone time to figure out the next step, if any, in their relationship. When she'd zipped up Peter's suitcase, she'd found the Cartier engagement ring he'd originally given her when she was a senior in high school. She'd kept the ring even after the engagement had been called off after her father's investment fraud scandal had erupted, an event that had upended her and her younger brother Wesley's lives. Evicted from their palatial home in the most toney section of Atlanta, they had moved into the small townhome in Lindbergh (a decidedly *less* toney section of town) where she and Wesley still lived.

Alone.

Because her father Randolph hadn't been man enough to face his day in court. Instead he and their mother Valerie had disappeared for over ten years, leaving her to raise her inconsolable little brother and fend for themselves. She'd been ill-prepared for the task, but somehow she and Wesley had muddled through, and their sibling bond was strong.

Last year she'd hocked the engagement ring to pay overdue bills, but Peter, who was single again and inching back into her life, had recovered the ring and told her he would hold it for her. Apparently he'd been planning to propose again while they were in Las Vegas.

Carlotta sighed. Poor Peter... he'd been so patient with her, and now his good intentions had been foiled again, this time by the appearance of a serial murderer intent on ending Carlotta's life, and the stunning *reappearance* of her long-lost father who'd saved her. But before she could ask Randolph Wren the thousands of questions she'd accumulated over the years (*How could you leave us? Where have you been? Where's our mother?*), Detective Jack Terry had placed the fugitive under arrest and hauled him away.

Come and see me, Sweetheart. We have a lot to talk about.

Instead she'd been whisked away to the hospital to have her sliced shoulder stitched and bandaged, and then there'd been the matter of locating Wesley and breaking the news that their M.I.A. parent had found his way home. She'd expected Wesley to react explosively, but he'd been strangely quiet, almost catatonic... like those awful days after her parents had first left. By then the hour had been late and she was woozy from painkiller and Jack had told her it would be better if she gave herself time to recover and to let the dust settle before she and Wesley visited Randolph in jail.

You've waited this long... another day or two won't change anything. Take your time and get your thoughts together, then you and Wesley can present a united front. Besides, don't you think your father deserves to sit and stew a while before his family rushes to his side?

Jack was right, damn him. He was always right.

She winced. Her shoulder was throbbing now. The painkiller had definitely worn off. She used her good arm to push up, then swung her legs over the side of the bed. She'd slept in yoga pants and a button-up shirt to accommodate her injury. A nightlight provided enough illumination for her to remove a tablet from a prescription bottle. She stood on wobbly legs and made her way to the bathroom for a glass of tepid water to chase it down.

A glance in the mirror made her gasp—she looked like hell, hollow-eyed and sallow. A lump of emotion lodged in her throat. Yesterday she had been happy...ish. The terror reign of The Charmed Killer had been behind her, for once Wesley had seemed to be on the right track, and her personal life was moving in some definable direction. In hindsight, it should have been a red flag, the happiness—a sign that something bad was about to happen. She had always envisioned her father's return as a joyful day... so why did she feel so thoroughly miserable?

She picked up a brush and pulled it through her long, dark hair, enjoying the slightly painful scrape of the boar bristle brush against her scalp. Her eyes welled until her reflection blurred, and a familiar knot tightened in her stomach—anger and resentment that her life had turned out this way. It wasn't the way it was supposed to be. If her father hadn't been accused of investment fraud, if he and her mother hadn't abandoned her and Wesley, she would've gone on to college as she'd planned and married Peter when their love was still young and their lives more simple. Instead, Peter had left her and she'd worked her way up the retail ranks at Neiman Marcus to make ends meet while trying to raise her little brother. If her parents hadn't left, Wesley would've grown into a confident genius and now would be tucked away in an ivy league college instead of being an uneducated, underemployed body mover with gambling debts, questionable friends, and a history of substance abuse.

She set aside the brush and blinked away the tears. For years she'd spun fantasies about what her life might've been like if it hadn't been derailed by her parents' actions. If she could forgive them for herself, she would never forgive them for what they'd done to Wesley. Their disappearance had left the nine-year-old heartbroken and bewildered. All the games and diversions she'd desperately invented couldn't fill the void.

Carlotta took a deep breath and exhaled slowly. It was a waste of time to think about what might have been.

She padded back to her bed, but she felt too restless to lie down. She probably should've taken Peter up on his offer to stay at his place last night, but on the heels of her father's return, she'd felt compelled to stay here with Wesley, and to ward off well-meaning interlopers. She and Wesley deserved privacy to absorb the latest development, and she wanted to be there for him when and if his emotional dam burst.

She hugged herself and glanced around the room, longing for a safe place to curl up and start to make peace with her past. The cramped townhome had never felt like a haven to her... it had always represented the place her family had been banished to, where their family had ultimately fallen apart. At this moment, she longed for something familiar, something to remind her of the last time her family had been happy and intact.

Her head turned toward the garage, as if she'd heard her name called. She pushed her feet into flip flops and slipped out of her room. Across the hall, Wesley's bedroom door was closed because of Carlotta's perpetual fear that his pet python Einstein would escape its tank and find her.

She stopped and listened at the door, then silently turned the knob and peeked inside, as she'd done thousands of times since he was little. Seeing her gangly brother sprawled innocently on his back in his boyhood bed, limbs flung wide, it was hard to imagine all the adult trouble he'd gotten himself into—arrested for hacking into the city courthouse computer, in debt to some of the nastiest loan sharks in town, a brush with oxycontin addiction. Her mouth turned down. And she didn't even want to think about his relationship to his much older attorney Liz Fischer, alleged friend of the family who, as it turned out, had been having an affair with her father before he left town and who had recently transferred her attention to Randolph's son. *Ugh.*

She only hoped that Wesley's crush on his coworker Meg would drive him from Liz's clutches. And at least he had Coop back.

Cooper Craft. Just the thought of the man who had taken Wesley under his wing made her smile. The fact that he'd given Wes a job as a body mover for the morgue hadn't set well with her in the beginning. But that was before she'd gotten to know the gentle, cerebral man and his story. Formerly the Medical Examiner for Fulton County, Georgia, he'd lost his job due to excessive drinking and relegated to a lowly contract position with the facility he had once overseen. But Coop was so appealing he'd even drawn Carlotta and her friend

Hannah into the body moving business. And he'd made no secret of the fact that he wanted to be more than friends with Carlotta.

But their timing had always been off. Conversely, she and Jack had amazing chemistry, but the man was an island. And through it all, Peter had been there, waiting for her to come to her senses, for them to begin the life they should've had all along.

From the bed, Wesley made a troubled noise. She started toward him, then stopped herself—he wasn't a child anymore. He quieted, and his breathing deepened. Satisfied, she backed out of his room and headed to the front door.

Her gaze landed on the tarnished metallic fringed Christmas tree in the corner, with its sad, faded little packages underneath. It had stood there since her parents had left—Wesley wouldn't let her open the gifts. He had imagined that one day their parents would just come home and they would just pick up where they'd left off.

Her hand tightened on the doorknob—she had to get out of this place.

She unlocked the door quietly and slipped outside by the glow of the dim light over the stoop. Dawn was still at least an hour away, but the city was already beginning to wake. Next door, the light in Mrs. Winningham's kitchen was on. Their nosy neighbor would no doubt be over fishing for details about their father's return as soon as she could throw together a casserole. She was probably at this moment opening a can of condensed cream of chicken soup and cubing Velveeta.

Carlotta descended the steps and made her way to the garage in the dim lighting. After a bit of wrestling, she managed to raise the door with her good arm. Inside sat the two-door rental car that Peter had secured for her since her blue Monte Carlo Super Sport had been blown to Kingdom Come. And next to the rental sat her beloved white Miata convertible.

Just the sight of it made her heart unfurl. Her father had bought her the car when she was still in high school, and she'd felt like a princess. When their charmed life had disintegrated around them, her parents had allowed her to keep the car. When they had disappeared, the little convertible was one of the few souvenirs from the time when she and her family had been happy. Climbing behind the wheel had always made her feel safe and loved.

She ran her hand over the sloping rear fender. A pang of sadness struck her when her hand came away with a thick coat of dust. The car hadn't run for some time now—she hadn't been able to afford repairs, but neither had she had the heart to sell it.

She opened the door and slid into the cool seat, comforted by the familiar hug of the caramel-colored leather. She closed the door and glanced around the interior, still in great shape. The console compartment revealed a hodge-podge of CDs and lip balm and ink pens. She removed a folded piece of yellow paper—the quote from the repair shop, she remembered as she opened it. The rather ominous-sounding engine parts needed had been itemized, with the caveat that the cooling system was perhaps "half" salvageable since one of the two fans worked.

She sighed. Six and a half body parts to get this baby running again... at a gut-clutching price she couldn't afford any time in the near future.

She dropped the quote back into the console and closed the lid. Impulsively, she placed her hands on the steering wheel for a squeeze. Like a time machine, the car took her back to a place when she was young and carefree, when her entire life extended before her, yet was pointed in a direction of happiness and success. She leaned her head back against the headrest and allowed the good memories to flood over her. Back then, her most pressing problems had been finding the right shade of nail polish, juggling social commitments, and making plans to join her fiancé Peter at Vanderbilt University when she graduated.

She smiled and her eyes fluttered shut as the images of her life as it was supposed to be spooled through her head—an unbroken family... college educated... married to Peter Ashford... rich and happy... it was an intoxicating dream.

When she started awake, daylight streamed into the garage through the open door. How long had she slept? She lifted her head and winced as stiff muscles protested. She had to get moving—today was an important day. She and Wesley needed to talk about Randolph and arrange to see him. She expected the press to descend at some point, and she'd rather not be found sitting in her crippled car, daydreaming.

She opened the door and climbed out, then did a double-take to see that the silver Honda rental that had been parked next to her had been replaced with a silver four-door Mercedes. She frowned in confusion, then reasoned that Peter might have arrived early to check on her, had probably arranged to return the rental car, and perhaps the Mercedes was his. Or maybe that piranha Liz Fischer was here. Of course she would've heard of Randolph's return by now, and of course, she'd come running.

Carlotta emerged from the garage and blinked at surroundings that were different... yet familiar. She stood and stared at the Buckhead home she and Wesley had grown up in, then shook her head in confusion. Had she somehow driven in a painkiller-induced haze to her childhood home? She walked closer, up the curved flagstone walkway, noting the details of the lush landscaping, the elaborate covered entryway leading to regal double-doors flanked by shining stained glass insets. She'd forgotten how truly beautiful the house was. She wondered with a pang who lived there now.

The thought still lingered in her mind when the front door opened and an elegantly-dressed woman emerged to scoop up the folded newspaper lying in front of the door.

Carlotta panicked, a lie already forming on her lips for when the woman demanded to know why she was standing in her yard. Instead, when the woman glanced up, a smile spread across her face.

"Carlotta? This is a nice surprise."

Carlotta's heart stopped. Her lungs froze. Her brain refused to register what her eyes were seeing. At last, her tongue loosened. *"Mother?"*

CHAPTER TWO

CARLOTTA STARED AT the woman she hadn't seen in more than ten years. Valerie Randolph had aged gracefully, her jet hair still convincingly dark, but cropped to her chin, her cheekbones still high and perhaps more chiseled, her brown eyes framed with enough lines to hint at experience. She remained tall and slender as ever. She wore a long black silky robe and matching mules, her taste as impeccable as Carlotta remembered.

Her mother gave a little laugh. "Are you okay? You look like you've seen a ghost."

"Where... where have you been?" Carlotta asked carefully.

A little wrinkle marred Valerie's brow. "It's been a busy week—I was at the club yesterday, and at the chiropractor the day before. Did I miss your call?"

Carlotta's mind raced. Valerie acted as if she had seen Carlotta mere days ago. At the time of her parents' disappearance, her mother had been a high-functioning alcoholic... perhaps she was living in her own reality.

"Yes," Carlotta murmured. "I was worried."

Valerie looked contrite. "I'm sorry. Do you need to tell me something?"

How about a million somethings? Maybe their old home was currently vacant. Maybe Valerie had returned to Atlanta with Randolph, and had taken up residence in the unoccupied home—hadn't she seen a news segment about evicted residents returning to their empty homes? Her mother's history with alcohol would explain such aberrant behavior.

Although it didn't explain how she herself had gotten here.

Valerie walked toward her, her expression one of concern. Carlotta stood rooted to the spot, fear rising in her chest as Valerie reached out to her, half expecting her mother's hand to pass through her. When her mother's fingers touched her arm, she marveled over the contact.

"Why don't you come inside, sweetheart." Valerie's voice sounded gentle, as if Carlotta was the unstable one.

Carlotta followed her into the house, steeled to see a vacant interior, fallen into disrepair. But when she walked over the threshold into the grand foyer that opened into rooms leading off in every direction, she was plunged headlong into her mother's decadent decorating style—Old World European. Heavy antiques, plush rugs, and luxurious fabrics furnished the rooms of the home she remembered. It was the same as when she'd lived here, only different. More... modern?

Valerie walked ahead toward the kitchen, as if nothing were amiss. Carlotta trailed after her, glancing around, noting objects she'd forgotten—the oil painting her parents had brought back from Italy, the Steuben glass dolphin her father's company Mashburn, Tully & Wren Investments, had given them for an anniversary. Carlotta reeled from sensory overload—none of this could be real.

So how could her nose be tickling from the cinnamon-orange scent that Valerie stocked in oil diffusers in every room?

Still, she'd bet the downstairs had been staged to sell the house—the rooms on the upper floors were probably bare.

Carlotta wanted to say something—to scream at the top of her lungs—and confront her mother about her unforgivable act of abandoning her children, but she was afraid to break the spell, afraid to trigger an episode if her mother was operating within the boundaries of a mental illness. And the compulsion to see how this bizarre encounter would play out was overwhelming.

"Cappuccino?" Valerie asked, breezing up to a state of the art beverage machine installed into one of the solid cherry cabinets. The kitchen had been updated to rival a commercial food preparation center.

"When did you start making morning coffee?" Carlotta asked, unable to keep the suspicious tone from her voice. Perpetually hung over, Valerie typically didn't put in an appearance until afternoon.

"Henny has the day off," Valerie said without missing a beat.

Henny, their former maid, Carlotta recalled. It was the first chink in her mother's story—she could pretend that she'd never left Atlanta, but when it came to other people who had once occupied the house, of course she would have to manufacture stories to explain their absence.

"Cappuccino, yes?" Valerie prompted.

"Just black coffee is fine."

"How was yoga, dear?"

"What?"

Valerie gestured to Carlotta's outfit. "I assume you went to an early yoga class."

"Oh... right. It was... fine."

"Did you and Peter have a fight?"

Carlotta frowned—her mother assumed she and Peter were still a couple? Her gaze darted to her left hand, but her finger was bare. Then she bit down on the inside of her cheek—she and Peter *were* still a couple... weren't they? "No, we didn't have a fight."

"Is your car acting up again?"

Carlotta pressed her lips together. "Yes. I need to put it in the shop."

Valerie shook her head, poured them both a cup of black coffee, and extended a mug to Carlotta. "I don't know why you insist on hanging on to that toy car."

"Because Daddy bought it for me," Carlotta said rather sharply. "It's special."

Valerie lifted her hand. "Far be it for me to get in the middle of you and your father." She turned her back to position herself between Carlotta and something she removed from a drawer, but Carlotta saw the bottle as Valerie poured two glugs of vodka into the coffee. Her mother was still drinking, but had found new ways to incorporate it into her schedule.

Carlotta opened her mouth to ask if Valerie happened to know that Randolph had been taken into custody, when the sound of someone jogging down the stairs made her turn her head. To her astonishment, Randolph himself burst into the kitchen in full stride. He wore a flawless gray suit, white shirt, and striped tie. He was a handsome ball of energy, fit and tanned. The gray at his temples lent a distinguished air to his boyish good looks. His grin took Carlotta's breath away. She was starting to think she'd stepped into the Twilight Zone.

"Hey, Sweetheart," he said, stopping long enough to drop a kiss on her cheek. "What brings you around so early? Did you and Peter have a fight?"

She frowned. "No."

"Good." Satisfied, he turned his attention to Valerie and her spiked java. "Starting the day off right, my dear?" His voice was laced with sarcasm.

She gave him a tight smile. "Just getting a head start on the celebration, *my dear.*"

Even with her mind racing a hundred miles an hour to figure out what was going on, Carlotta couldn't miss the undercurrent of hostility between her parents. Whatever alternate reality she'd entered, *that* hadn't changed.

"What celebration?" she asked.

"Peter didn't tell you?" Valerie said.

"Peter doesn't know," Randolph said.

"Know what?" Carlotta asked.

"Your father is going to be named president of the firm today." Valerie's voice was a mixture of pride and something else—resignation?

"That's wonderful, D-Daddy," Carlotta said, stumbling over the word that was rusty on her tongue.

He smiled, obviously pleased himself. "Thanks, Sweetheart. The office is having a little cocktail party at five o'clock—stop by if you like."

She could only nod.

"Gotta run," Randolph said, lifting his coffee cup toward Valerie in lieu of a kiss.

"Say hi to Liz Fischer for me," Valerie said sweetly.

Under his tan, Randolph blanched. "Liz?"

Valerie picked up his phone from the counter. "It beeped with a reminder that you're seeing her at noon."

"Right," he said smoothly, reaching for his phone. "To go over the new employment contract the firm drew up." As if to punctuate his fidelity, he stepped forward to kiss her mother, but Carlotta didn't miss Valerie's last minute head turn that resulted in the kiss landing on her chin.

"Okay, then," Randolph said cheerfully. "I'll see you both later."

Carlotta opened her mouth to say something—anything—to her father, to demand to know what the heck was going on and why he and her mother were both acting as if nothing was wrong, but she was confused. Her father was under arrest—she'd seen Jack handcuff him and haul him away with her own eyes... so how could he be standing here in the kitchen of the home she'd grown up in, as if they'd never left?

As if they'd never left.

She'd wondered and wished to know and experience what her life would've been like if her father hadn't been accused of investment fraud, if he and her mother hadn't abandoned her and Wesley... was this her wish being answered?

While her mind whirled in bewildered revelation, her father walked out the door whistling. Valerie took a hefty drink of her coffee, then gave Carlotta a shaky smile. "Don't you miss this happy family morning ritual?"

"Actually," Carlotta murmured, "I do."

Valerie angled her head. "What's wrong, dear?"

Only everything. "I guess I'm just feeling out of sorts today."

Her mother made a rueful noise. She reached out to stroke Carlotta's hair back from her face, resurrecting memories of when she was a little girl. "You do look different—tanned. You know the sun is bad for your skin."

"I just feel flushed," Carlotta said, conceding she hadn't been diligent about applying sunscreen as her mother had drilled into her head since she was a preteen.

"And your hair looks so much longer—did you get extensions?"

"No."

Valerie shook her head as if to clear the cobwebs. "I could've sworn... well, never mind, it suits you." She took another drink from her mug, then brightened. "How about some breakfast?"

Carlotta had never seen her mother turn on the stove, but she was hungry, and she wanted to prolong her visit. "How about a bagel?"

"You're eating carbs again?" Valerie squinted. "Are you pregnant?"

Carlotta's eyes flew wide. "What? No!"

"Just checking," Valerie said in a sing-songy voice. She opened six cabinets before she found a bag of bagels, emerging triumphant. She pulled out a bagel and dropped the halves into a toaster.

"Aren't you going to have one?" Carlotta prodded, thinking the bread would help to soak up the alcohol.

Valerie waved her hand. "You know I only eat one meal a day."

Yes, she remembered… and the meal usually consisted of a sparse green salad. Valerie enjoyed her reputation for being famously thin among her circle of friends at the club.

From the counter, the cordless phone trilled. Valerie glanced at the caller ID screen. "Oh, that's Bette calling about our fundraiser, I should take this. I'll keep an eye on your bagel. Do you mind running upstairs to try to get your brother out of bed?"

Carlotta couldn't contain her surprise. "Wesley is upstairs?"

Valerie gave a dry laugh as she reached for the handset. "Of course. And he needs to be somewhere in thirty minutes."

"Okay," Carlotta said, shot through with curiosity. She slowly walked toward the rear stairway, and tentatively set a foot on the bottom step. When it didn't disappear out from under her, she continued to climb.

If her parents hadn't left and life had gone on as planned, how had Wesley turned out?

CHAPTER THREE

AS CARLOTTA CLIMBED THE STAIRS to the second level of the home she'd grown up in, memories rolled over her. Framed chronological photographs of her and Wesley hung on the stairwell walls... she remembered that Easter bonnet, that Christmas dress. Wesley's mischievous smile shined back at her. The photographs continued at the top of the landing, and one in particular caused Carlotta to stop.

In the picture, she stood in the foreground of a party wearing a short yellow dress. The cake on the table in front of her read "Happy Graduation, Carlotta!" along with the year she'd graduated from high school. By the time she'd graduated from high school, though, her parents had fled. There had been no party, no dress. She had zero recollection of this event, or of the picture being taken.

With her heart pounding against her breastbone, she scoured the photos that followed: A picture of her in cap and gown. From her cap dangled a tassel in Vandy's school colors of black and gold.

She smiled in revelation—she was a college graduate. She desperately wished she could remember the experience. *What did I major in? Was I a good student or did I goof-off and squander the opportunity?*

There was a photo of Wesley as a teenager—she leaned closer—wrestling? It was hard to picture her braniac brother as being a jock. And another of him in a tux standing next to a blonde with cheerleader written all over her. He looked... cocky? Her myopic, quiet little brother who had been bullied in school and who to this day betrayed his insecurities with unwitting stabs to his glasses?

And why was there no photo of Wesley graduating high school?

Then she caught herself—she wasn't even sure what year this was… or was supposed to be. She glanced around for some sort of reference, and spied a digital infinity clock on a table in the hallway. When she saw the year was the current year, a chill ran down her spine.

She'd been so quick to assign a mental deficiency to Valerie, but was it possible that she was the crazy one? That she had dreamed up the scenario of her parents leaving to protect her from facing some other traumatic event? Something that she herself had caused. She'd read about people having psychotic breaks… it would explain why Valerie had been treating her with kid gloves since she'd "arrived" this morning.

The sound of loud snoring filtered out into the hallway. She turned her head in the direction of Wesley's room, then made her way over. Gingerly, she lifted her hand and knocked. When she received no response, she knocked harder. Suddenly, the snoring stopped.

"Go the hell away!" Wesley shouted.

Carlotta frowned. Wesley could be difficult, but he'd never been mean. For all he knew, Valerie was probably the one knocking, and since when did he think he could talk to his mother like that?

"Wes, open up," she called.

"Carlotta?" he shouted. "What the fuck do you want?"

She blinked, then frowned. "Mom wants you to get up."

"Go away."

After nearly a minute of silence, she pounded on the door.

"What?" he screamed.

Her head went back at the raw fury in his voice. Who did the little shithead think he was? "Get your butt out of bed… *now.*"

She heard the muffled sounds of him moving around and talking under his breath. The door opened and he stood there in a pair of Hanro micro boxer briefs. With a salon-tan and muscles in places she'd never seen on him. Even with bedhead, she could tell his hair was cut in a trendy style. "What?" he yelled.

Carlotta scowled at this almost unrecognizable version of her brother. "Since when do you wear skivvies that cost fifty bucks a pop?"

"Since when do you call Valerie 'mom'?" he sneered.

Anger rolled off him in waves. "You're supposed to be someplace in thirty minutes?" she prompted.

He turned back to his room. "What do you care?"

She followed him inside as he pulled on flashy designer jeans that the Wesley she knew wouldn't be caught dead in. "Try me."

"It's a damn tutoring session," he barked.

She straightened. "Oh. Who are you tutoring?"

He turned to glare at her. "Very funny. As if I could tutor anyone. I'm failing English—remember? For the second time."

She scoffed. "But you're a straight-A student, and English is your best subject."

He gave a harsh laugh. "You been drinking Valerie's coffee?"

She did some quick mental math and a troubling realization dawned. "You haven't graduated from high school yet."

He gave her a mean smile. "Yeah, rub it in. You, the girl who majored in pot and booze at Vandy. Did you even open that little tube they handed you at graduation to make sure there was a diploma inside?"

So she *had* wasted her chance for an education. The knowledge brought tears to her eyes. Her throat convulsed, then she angled her head. "Where are your glasses?" Maybe his academic issues could be remedied with something as simple as updated lenses.

"Duh... I got Lasik, remember? Did you get knocked on the head? You're acting retarded."

"That's not very nice."

He snorted. "Since when is our family nice?" He picked up a T-shirt and sniffed it, then pulled it over his head.

Carlotta glanced around his room, appalled at the number of naked pinup posters of some rather crude-looking women having some rather lewd things done to them. She knew her brother wasn't a virgin, but he'd always been respectful and discreet. What teenager displayed such misogyny in his parents' home?

"Where is Einstein?" she asked, glancing around.

"Who?"

"Your snake, silly."

"Snake? Are you insane?" A thumping ringtone with offensive lyrics burst into the room. He jammed his phone to his ear. "Yo… Yeah, I got some lame shit to take care of this morning, then I'll call you. Later."

Carlotta arched an eyebrow. "Let me guess—Chance Hollander?"

Wes made a face. "Hollander? Why would I be talking to that fat-ass loser nobody?"

She started to remind him that Chance was his best friend, but realized that this Wesley with the I'm-all-that attitude hadn't connected with the idle-minded but good-hearted frat boy who until this moment, Carlotta had only tolerated. But Chance was starting to look downright charming compared to the hateful brat in front of her.

"That was Zeph," he supplied.

"Who?"

He gave her a pointed look. "Zephyr—my girlfriend?"

Carlotta gave a wry laugh. "Zephyr? What is she, a stripper?"

"Uh, *yeah*."

Carlotta gasped. "Mom and Dad are letting you date a *stripper*?"

"You're kidding, right? Jesus, it's my life."

She crossed her arms. "You're still in high school and still living under their roof."

"Who are you and what have you done with my long-lost sister?"

She frowned. "What's that supposed to mean?"

He flailed his arms. "You left home and never looked back, left me here with these two misfits and now you think you can come around and try to be my mother?"

He felt as if she'd abandoned him. Where did she live now? With Peter? Something on Wesley's arm snagged her attention. She grabbed his wrist and stared at the red marks in the crook of his elbow. "What is this?"

He tried to twist away from her, but she held on with an iron grip. "Are these track marks?"

"Let go!" he wailed.

"Answer me!"

He wrenched his arm away. "Mind your own damn business."

She was so scared for him, her heart galloped in her chest. "What are you shooting up? Cocaine? Heroin?"

He leaned forward until his face was inches from hers. "What a hypocrite you are. Peter has snorted more coke up his nose than a rock star."

She stumbled backward. "Peter?"

Wes laughed. "As if you didn't know. Now get out of my room!" He put his palm on her chest and backed her out into the hallway, then slammed the door in her face.

Carlotta stood there, shaking, trying to digest everything she'd just learned about her brother... and Peter... and herself.

"Carlotta?" her mother called up the stairs.

She walked over to grip the stair railing and found her voice. "Yes?"

"Everything okay up there?" Valerie's lilting voice indicated she was sure that was the case, regardless of the commotion.

"Yes," Carlotta said, forcing a light tone. "Everything's fine."

And suddenly, it all came back to her full-force, how her family had communicated in trite phrases and air kisses and double entendres, like her parents' earlier conversation about Liz Fischer. No wonder Wesley had blown up when she pointed out the needle marks on his arms—they had been raised to believe that if you didn't say it aloud, it didn't exist.

"Good," Valerie said cheerfully. "By the way, I found that thing you asked me about. It's in your room."

She started to ask what thing, but the *tap, tap* of Valerie's mules indicated she'd already walked away. Carlotta turned her head to look farther down the hall, to the closed door to her own childhood bedroom. Dread washed over her. What would she find inside?

CHAPTER FOUR

CARLOTTA WAS IN A FLOP SWEAT by the time she reached the door of her former bedroom. She had the uneasy feeling she might find herself inside.

She turned the knob and pushed open the door noiselessly—she'd kept the hinges oiled so she could more easily slip in and out of her room with no one the wiser. She winced, conceding that she'd been a bit of a wild child before her parents' disappearance had forced her to grow up in a hurry.

The first thing she zeroed in on was the white bed—the same bed she'd crawled out of this morning in the townhome. A cold awareness settled over her as she struggled to stay vertical. Here was solid proof that she was walking in some kind of alternate universe, where people and things were on a trajectory separate from the world she knew.

The air inside was stale, as if the bedroom hadn't been used in a while. Most of her girly things had been removed—the comforter and window coverings were new and gender neutral, but there were still a few familiar knick-knacks here and there. She walked around, trailing her fingers over the furniture, then moved to the wide picture window overlooking the front yard.

How many times had she stood here waiting for Peter's car to arrive, usually in the dark. He would flash his lights once to signal her. She would rush down to slip into the Crown Victoria, his father's old car, too big to be cool, but sporting a back seat as expansive as a full-size bed. She and Peter would drive to some secluded spot and get wrapped up in each other. Just the memory of it sent a tug of longing through her midsection. That was back when sex was new and exciting and a little scary... they had spent hours kissing and caressing and exploring each other's bodies. She had been so in love... she thought

Peter had been, too. But her father's scandal had been enough to cause him to reconsider their future together. He had turned his back on her when she'd needed him most.

She roused herself from the past before she became mired in the murkiness. Her mother had said she'd asked her to find something. She glanced around the room, looking for an item that stood out. On the edge of a dresser lay a small yellow photo album. The cover read "My College Graduation" written in block letters in her handwriting.

She opened it and recognized herself in cap and gown, and the yellow dress and the cake from the photograph on the hallway wall. She flipped through the photos, studying the candids of herself and what she presumed were other students she hung around with. A few faces were familiar—Peter, of course, and fellow high school mates Tracey Tully and Angela Ashford—correction, Angela Keener. Carlotta bit her lip. If she and Peter were together, apparently he hadn't married Angela. Did that mean the woman was still alive?

The impact of being here, on a parallel path, hit her… what might she find if she kept going? How different was her life in this other place?

She flipped through the rest of the photos, but she had no recollection of the other people. She felt a pang for the good time she'd obviously had but couldn't remember. Then she frowned.

Why had she asked her mother to locate the album?

"Did you find the pictures?" Valerie yelled from downstairs.

Carlotta closed the photo album and walked toward the hall. "Yes."

"Your bagel is ready," Valerie said, her voice muffled.

Carlotta turned to take another look at her childhood room, remembering the happy times here—the endless fashion shows, the impromptu dancing, the hushed phone calls. She had been so spoiled, and blissfully ignorant of how drastically her life could change overnight. She pulled the door closed, then made her way back to the stairs. Obnoxious music leaked out of Wesley's bedroom door. She wondered what he was doing in there, thinking it probably wasn't good.

She descended the stairs with a stone in her stomach, wondering what else she might find out about her family and herself. This was starting to feel uncomfortably voyeuristic.

She returned to the kitchen to find Valerie humming and sipping from a coffee mug that had been refilled with her "special" brew.

"Thanks," she said, lifting the photo album.

"You're welcome," Valerie said, glancing at the album as if she'd never seen it before.

It occurred to Carlotta that her mother had probably asked Henny to find the photo album—Valerie had a tendency to offload any parenting duties she could.

"Wesley's up," Carlotta offered.

"Oh, good."

"Mom, I'm worried about him. He seems so... angry."

"Angry? Why would he be angry?"

Carlotta pressed her lips together. "Have you ever found drugs in his room?"

"Of course not!"

"Have you ever looked?"

Valerie made an exasperated noise. "Why would I do that?"

"Mother," Carlotta said sternly, "I think you need to keep a closer eye on Wes, maybe occasionally ask him what's going on in his life. Do you know he's dating a stripper?"

"That will pass, dear. He's at that age where he's curious—about a lot of things."

Carlotta crossed her arms. "Ergo the saying that curiosity killed the cat."

"Nonsense."

"Mother, I really think—"

"Carlotta," Valerie cut in sharply, "I think I know more about mothering than you do."

Carlotta felt as if she'd been slapped. She wanted to fling back that she'd known nothing about mothering when Randolph and Valerie had skipped town, but she'd had to sink or swim and deal with Wesley's grief and confusion and nightmares, getting him transferred to public school and generally trying to make him feel loved and safe in an impossible situation. Hot tears formed in her eyes as spiteful words watered on her tongue... and died there.

Because she'd waited for this moment for so long, to be standing in front of her mother, that she wanted to drink her in and let their time together be a happy occasion. Besides, in this version of their life, it probably did seem to Valerie as if she was interfering.

She blinked away the tears before her mother could notice. "You're right. I'm just worried about him, that's all."

Valerie looked up and Carlotta detected a flash of clarity in her mother's eyes. "If you must know, so am I," Valerie said quietly, as if she were afraid the walls were listening. "I'll talk to your father about it this evening, after the cocktail party." She took another drink from her mug, signaling an end to the topic, but Carlotta felt somewhat better.

She picked up the bagel, noting that Valerie had spread it with her favorite, strawberry preserves. The little motherly gesture touched her, reminded her that Valerie wasn't without her good qualities. She bit into her bagel and chewed slowly, wondering when the bubble around her would burst and she would be bounced back into life as she knew it. This all seemed so surreal, yet her senses were more keen—she could hear the second hand moving on the ornate clock above the door, could taste the caramel in the coffee. A blob of jelly dropped onto her shirt, and the stain was the brightest red.

"By the way, Bette asked me to say hello."

Carlotta turned her head. "Hm?"

"That was Bette Noble on the phone... from the club? She wondered how your police benefit is shaping up."

"Police benefit?" Carlotta parroted, stalling.

"To raise money for bulletproof vests. Bette organized it last year, remember?"

Carlotta vaguely remembered the woman's name, but couldn't picture her face. "Right. Tell Bette it's going... fine."

"She said she was in Dahlonega the other day having lunch with her sister and ran into Peter."

Carlotta didn't know if or why Peter would be in a small town an hour north of the city. "That's nice. More coffee?" she asked, offering to top off her mother's mug.

Valerie looked trapped, then extended her mug. "Just a little."

Carlotta filled the mug to the brim.

Her mother frowned into her cup. "How are the renovations going?"

Carlotta arched an eyebrow. "Renovations?"

"On the house, dear."

Carlotta's mind immediately went to the renovations she wanted to do to the townhouse... but her mother had to be talking about something else. Did she have her own home? If so, how had she afforded it? Did she still work at Neiman Marcus? Had she trained for a career other than retail in college? Did she live with Peter?

"Fine," she murmured.

The chime of the doorbell sounded. Carlotta's pulse pounded at the thought of confronting someone else she knew from her other life. "Wonder who that could be?"

"It's Peter," Valerie said matter-of-factly.

"Peter?" Her pulse skyrocketed.

"He called and asked if you were here. Apparently, you left your phone at home. I told him you were having car trouble."

"Oh."

The doorbell chimed again, this time more insistently. When Carlotta remained frozen, Valerie angled her head. "Honestly, dear, you're behaving so strangely today. Aren't you going to let Peter in?"

"Uh... sure." Carlotta's feet felt like bricks as she dragged herself toward the door. She had been able to pass herself off as the "old" Carlotta to her family, but Peter would know she was... different.

Besides, she hadn't a clue where things stood between the two of them.

This should be interesting.

CHAPTER FIVE

CARLOTTA STOPPED IN FRONT of the door and took a deep breath, wondering how she was expected to greet Peter—it was apparent her family thought they were together in some capacity, but to what extent... and was she happy about it?

She swung open the door to find Peter standing there, tall and blond and handsome, tucking his phone into the inside pocket of an immaculate jacket.

"Hi." He stepped toward her and lowered a tentative kiss near her mouth.

"Hi," she said, wondering why he seemed as nervous as she felt.

"You forgot your phone," he said, then pulled a sleek model with a pink case from another pocket and extended it to her.

"Thank you," she murmured, comparing the up-to-the-minute smart phone to the one she was accustomed to using. She wasn't even sure how to turn it on.

She looked up at Peter and studied his face, noting small changes—a pinch around his mouth, a tic at his temple. His hair was just as fair, but perhaps sporting more "product." His suit was dark and his tie, authoritative, befitting his position of investment broker—assuming he had followed the same path, working at Mashburn, Tully & Wren Investments.

He angled his head. "You look... different. Did you get hair extensions?"

"No."

He squinted. "Hm... I can't put my finger on it. What's that?" He gestured to the yellow photo album she held and she noticed he wasn't wearing a wedding ring... so apparently they weren't married.

Why did that thought buoy her?

"These are just pictures from my college graduation party."

"Why do you suddenly want those?"

She was caught off guard by the suspicious tone in his voice. "Just feeling nostalgic, I guess."

"Are you ready?" he asked abruptly.

She blinked, realizing he expected her to leave with him. "To go where?"

He arched an eyebrow. "To Neiman's. Don't you have a meeting?"

Although she was relieved to hear she was still doing something familiar, she glanced down at her casual yoga pants, shirt, and flip-flops. "I'm not exactly dressed for it."

He gave her a wry smile. "So for once you have a good excuse to buy something when you get there."

She smiled—this man knew her, no matter what universe they were in. Then her smile fell.

"What's wrong?" he asked.

"Nothing." Carlotta looked over her shoulder, reluctant to leave after spending such little time with her mother. "I just need to say goodbye to Mom."

He looked surprised. "You and Valerie must be having a good visit if you're calling her 'Mom.' Okay, I'll wait in the car."

She watched him walk back to his navy blue Porsche sitting in the driveway. She pursed her mouth—apparently in this world, she hadn't totaled his beloved car like she had in the other. Turning back to the foyer, she moved toward the kitchen with leaden feet. She didn't want to go. When she entered the kitchen, Valerie had her back to the doorway, and seemed to be staring into space.

"Mom?" Carlotta said tentatively.

Valerie turned around and smiled. "Yes, dear?"

"I'm going… with Peter."

"Okay." Valerie said it as if her daughter's leaving were no big deal… as if it hadn't been and wouldn't be another decade before they saw each other again.

Carlotta wanted to run into her mother's arms and bury her face in her neck and never let go. Instead she walked up and gave her a hug, stepping back when Valerie released her first. "Will I see you again soon?" She couldn't help the wistful tone in her voice.

Valerie looked perplexed. "Aren't you coming to the cocktail party this evening?"

"Oh… right."

"Okay then. Have a good day." Valerie fluttered her fingers in a wave, then picked up the telephone, her mind already elsewhere.

Cheered at the promise of more family contact, Carlotta backed out of the kitchen and left the house, but still felt a panicky loss when she closed the door behind her. She walked slowly toward Peter's car, wondering if everything would collapse and she would be catapulted back to where she'd come from if she stepped outside the perimeter of the property.

Peter stuck his head out of the window, his expression impatient. "Come on, we're both going to be late."

She picked up the pace, and gingerly climbed into the passenger seat of the car that no longer existed in the other world. "Your car looks good."

He gave a little laugh as he steered through the streets of the posh neighborhood that was beginning to wake up. "Is that a hint you're finally ready for a grown up car?"

She frowned. "And get rid of my Miata?"

"Jesus, Carly, it's on its last wheel. Let it go."

"But I love that car."

"I know, but one of these days it's going to leave you broken down someplace more dangerous than your parents' garage."

She held herself very still and studied his profile, still marveling over her predicament, and hearing Wesley's words about Peter's drug use echo in her head.

"Is something on my face?" he asked.

"What?"

"You're staring. Or is something on your mind?"

"No," she said quickly, then added, "Should there be?"

"Nope." But he leaned forward to fidget with the stereo settings, and she thought again that he seemed nervous. Was he picking up on the fact that she wasn't the same person she'd been the last time he'd seen her?

She was afraid to say something that might sound strange, so she busied herself with the phone Peter had handed her, tabbing through the contacts folder, trying to get some insight into this version of herself. Alarm bubbled in her stomach at the unfamiliar names... and the absence of others. Where was Hannah's number? And Jack's? And Coop's?

When her anxiety pushed her heart rate higher, she set down the phone and looked out the car window. The landscape, at least, was familiar. They left the gated community where she'd grown up and merged into rush hour traffic stuttering in both directions—she never thought she would find the crush of traffic so comforting. As they inched toward the Lenox shopping area where Neiman's and the offices of Mashburn, Tully & Wren were located, she noticed a few differences—mostly eateries that had changed names, and her favorite bookstore was now a coffee shop.

They were sitting at a complete standstill and Peter's patience was wearing thin. He kept pulling out his phone to check for a message that, judging from his frown, hadn't yet arrived. Neither did he seem to be in a talkative mood, and Carlotta suddenly wondered what they talked about.

"How are things at the office?" she asked.

"Fine."

"Daddy told me he's going to be named president today."

That got his attention. "Really?" His mouth pulled downward. "Funny, Randolph didn't mention it to me."

"I guess it was a secret."

His hands gripped the steering wheel tighter. "Plenty of those around the office, for sure."

She frowned. "What's that supposed to mean?"

"Oh, you know... office politics." He pulled his hand down his face, then checked his phone again. "I'd rather not talk about it."

"Okay. But he said there would be a cocktail party this evening and he invited me."

"By all means, come." But his voice was curt and his mind was elsewhere—and obviously not in a happy place.

Carlotta wet her lips. "Peter, if something at work is bothering you, you can tell me."

But at the way his jaw tightened, she got the feeling he didn't believe her.

"I won't say anything to my father," she added, disappointed that it apparently needed to be said.

He turned to look at her and the expression in his eyes told her that something was indeed troubling him. Just when she thought he was going to say something, the moment passed. He looked away and his mouth tightened. "Call me if you need a ride to the office this evening. Do you want me to have the convertible towed?"

"No, I'll take care of it," she said, unwilling to hand off responsibility for the car that delivered her here.

Casting about for another topic of conversation, she picked up the photo album in her lap. "I don't even remember this party," she ventured.

Peter glanced at the photos. "No surprise. You killed a lot of brain cells back then."

So Wesley was right about her being a party animal in college... was he also right about other things?

She flipped through the photos slowly, scrutinizing herself, and the body language of people around her. Peter wasn't standing close to her in any of the pictures, nor was he looking at her, even when everyone else was. Curious.

"Peter, do you like me?"

The car lurched as he stabbed the brake. He jerked his head toward her. "What?"

"Do you like me... this way?"

He looked confused. "What way?"

"The way I am."

He blanched, then tried to laugh as he looked back to the traffic. "What's with you today?"

"Just answer the question."

"Of course I like you this way. It's the way you are."

"And how are *we*, Peter?"

His laugh was a few seconds too late and a little too loud as he turned into the upscale shopping center. "What kind of question is that? This ring business is messing with your head."

She schooled her face. "What ring business?"

"Don't be coy. I know you've been upset about us not wearing our rings."

Her mind pinged frantically. What rings?

He pulled up in front of the Neiman Marcus entrance, put the car into Park, then leaned over to open the glove compartment. "I was going to surprise you later. I picked them up early." He removed two Cartier ring boxes. He opened the first one to reveal two thick gold bands.

Her heart jumped in her chest. "Wedding rings?" she squeaked.

"Newly buffed and cleaned," he said. He removed the smaller band and slipped it onto her ring finger, then removed the larger one and put it on his own long finger. "There," he said. "Back where they belong."

She gave him a tremulous smile, reeling over the implication of the unaccustomed weight on her finger.

"And," he said, opening the second box, "happy anniversary."

She stared at the familiar diamond cluster ring—it was the original Cartier solitaire engagement ring, sporting the addition of a diamond on either side… just as he'd done in the *other* world.

"I thought it was time to upgrade your engagement ring," he said.

"It's beautiful," she murmured, still trying to get used to the idea that she and Peter were married. Did it count if she couldn't remember it?

"Aren't you going to try it on?"

With a shaking hand, she removed the ring and pushed it onto her finger, snug against her wedding band. The three large stones shimmered back at her. "It's… " *Terrifying.* "Perfect." She smiled, realizing for whatever time she was here, she had to fit into this life… and try to make it better. "Thank you, Peter."

He seemed to relax—had the awkwardness she'd felt between them simply been his nervous anticipation of unveiling the surprise? He was so thoughtful. She leaned forward to kiss him, and he seemed so startled, she wondered how long it had been since they'd kissed like this? She put her hand around the nape of his neck and slanted her mouth over his, wanting to prove to herself that she'd made good choices in this version of her life, that she loved this man.

When she lifted her head, desire flashed in his blue eyes. "Wow. Who are you and what have you done with my wife?"

She laughed, squashing a guilty pang, then gestured toward the store entrance. "I guess I'd better get to work."

It was his turn to laugh. "Work—right... good one. Although I'd probably be money ahead if you had a Neiman's employee discount."

She balked and started to ask why she was there when her phone beeped. On the screen was an appointment reminder "meet T @ NM to discuss police benefit."

Okay... but who was T?

"There's Tracey now," Peter said with a nod, answering her unspoken question.

Carlotta looked up to see her nemesis, Tracey Tully Lowenstein, walking toward her, waving like mad. The reigning mean queen of their private school and later, the country club, had made Carlotta's life a living hell after her parents had absconded, taking the family's social status with them. The blonde bitch and her cronies loved to come in to Neiman Marcus and have Carlotta wait on them.

"Oh, shit," she muttered.

"What's wrong?" Peter asked.

Her mind spun. "I... forgot my purse."

He smiled. "I know—at home. I thought you might need it." He reached into the cubbyhole behind her seat and pulled out a Bottega Veneta pink leather hobo bag.

Carlotta pursed her mouth. At least she had good taste in handbags in this world. "Thank you," she said, longing for a few moments of privacy to go through its contents to perhaps find out more about her life. Instead she slipped the phone and photo album inside and tried to gather her wits.

"See you later?" Peter asked, sounding hopeful.

"Definitely," Carlotta said, then gave him another kiss before hopping out of the car. She waved as he pulled away, straining against the weight of his rings on her hand.

"Carlotta! *Hell-lo-oo!*"

Carlotta swallowed and steeled herself to face her "friend" Tracey, reminding herself that this was her life.

CHAPTER SIX

"HI, TRACEY," Carlotta said, manufacturing a smile for the woman who had made her life miserable for more than a decade. Her marriage to a successful doctor had further fueled her sense of entitlement.

Tracey leaned forward to deliver air kisses to both cheeks, then stood back and surveyed Carlotta's outfit. "You look great, as always, but a little casual for a presentation, don't you think?"

Presentation? Carlotta's pulse blipped. "I had car trouble this morning after yoga class... I was planning to buy something here to improvise."

"Of course," Tracey said with a wave, then she squinted. "Your hair looks longer... did you get extensions?"

"No."

"Liar, but they look good. And whatever makeup you're using is nice—you look tanned and natural."

"Er, thanks."

"Oh, my God!" She snatched up Carlotta's left hand. "When did you get the giant diamond upgrade?"

Carlotta's cheeks warmed. "Peter gave it to me just before he dropped me off."

Tracey pursed her mouth. "Sounds like a guilt gift to me—maybe your suspicions were correct."

"About?"

"About the fact that Peter is involved with something—or someone—he shouldn't be."

The pronouncement sent her stomach plummeting—what was going on in her marriage?

Tracey gave her a sympathetic look, then glanced at her watch. "We can talk about it later. We only have thirty minutes before the meeting, so let's get you dressed."

Carlotta followed Tracey to the entrance, wondering what she was walking into. "Um, in your opinion, what do we need to accomplish at this meeting?"

"You said yourself the other day—if we walk away with the decision made as to which model of bulletproof vest we're going to order for the APD, that will be a huge accomplishment.

It's taken us ages to get to this point."

Carlotta hoped she wasn't expected to go into the meeting with some type of prior knowledge. Her main experience with the APD was pleading Wesley's case and generally staying out of Jack Terry's way. She realized with a start that in this life, Randolph wasn't a fugitive and Wesley hadn't been arrested for computer hacking, so she wouldn't have crossed paths with Jack.

A fact that bothered her more than it should since the absence of Jack in her life meant she and her family were leading a normal, law-abiding existence.

Which was good… right?

She and Tracey rode upstairs to the Misses designer section, which looked very much like it had on her last day of work, whenever that had been. She had a specific jacket in mind, if this Neiman's had it in stock.

"Oh, look, there's Patricia Alexander," Tracey said, her voice gleeful—and mean. "Talk about someone who peaked in high school."

Carlotta looked up to see the tall blonde she worked with. They'd gotten off on shaky footing because Patricia's family moved in the same social circle as Tracey's, and Patricia had made sly remarks regarding Randolph's scandal. But over time Carlotta had begun to suspect that Patricia's job at Neiman's wasn't simply to fight boredom as she'd first professed, and that she lashed out because her own family had fallen on rough financial times. Over time the women had reached a tolerant alliance… Carlotta had even come to realize that the younger woman looked up to her.

"Be nice," Carlotta admonished. "She's just trying to make a living."

Tracey arched an eyebrow. "Well, look at you being all charitable."

Carlotta didn't respond, and felt a stab of remorse at the expression on Patricia's face when she saw them coming—part fear, part resigned politeness.

"Hello, ladies," she said, as if arming herself. "May I help you find something?"

"Hi, Patricia," Carlotta said, giving the woman a smile. "I'm in a pinch and need to dress up my outfit. I saw a St. John jacket earlier—it's turquoise and has a ruffled front. Do you still have it?"

"Yes," Patricia said warily. "If you'd like to try it on, I'll bring it to the dressing room."

"That would be nice, thank you." She moved toward the dressing room with Tracey on her heels. "Remind me, where is this meeting?"

"Upstairs, in the conference room."

"Right. And how is Neiman's involved?"

"Duh... they're kicking in matching funds. And they secured samples from the manufacturers of the bullet proof vests." She angled her head. "Are you okay to attend this meeting? You're acting strange."

"I'm just feeling a little off-kilter today."

"Car trouble will do that to you. Maybe now you'll get rid of that Hello Kitty convertible."

"Maybe."

In the lobby of the dressing room, Carlotta studied her reflection in a three-way mirror—long dark hair, deep brown eyes, gapped front teeth. She apparently still looked enough like herself to pass as herself, which was comforting—even with Peter's money at her disposal, she hadn't succumbed to the temptation to tweak her face or her body. Yet it was becoming more clear that the woman staring back at her, whose life had apparently bumped along as planned, was not entirely happy.

"Here we are," Patricia said cheerfully, laden with merchandise. She hung two of the requested turquoise jackets on a rack outside a dressing room which she unlocked with a fluid motion. "I brought different sizes of the jacket, plus some belts and shoes for you to try, if you like."

Good girl, Carlotta thought. *Way to upsell.* "Thank you." She looked over the items and checked the price tags, sobering when she remembered she wouldn't be getting her employee discount. Then just as quickly, she realized she probably had a deck of credit cards in her wallet. She felt a rush of power and freedom she hadn't experienced her entire adult life... people who said money couldn't buy happiness had never worried about how to make their little brother's bail.

Or pay his loan sharks.

She pulled on one of the jackets, gratified at the slide of the sumptuous fabric that draped and flattered. A wide silver-tone link belt added polish to her long shirt, and a Fendi black and cognac high-heeled leather sandal replaced the flip-flops.

"I'll take these," she said to Patricia, who looked relieved and supplied scissors to remove price tags.

Carlotta withdrew a Chanel wallet from the purse Peter had given her. As expected, she had to sort through several specialty credit cards before she found her Neiman's plastic. But it was jarring to see the name Carlotta Ashford printed on each of them. Her chest twinged for the loss of Carlotta Wren.

"Not bad," Tracey said, nodding at the outfit. Then she pursed her mouth. "You got a brush in your purse?"

Carlotta leaned closer to the mirror, conceding she looked a little wallowed from her trip. Inside the purse, she found, among other things, an iPad—she was a chic geek?—plus a hairbrush and a tube of lipstick. She made quick repairs, wondering how long she'd be able to masquerade as herself. When she signed the sales receipt, she gave Patricia a warm smile and thanked her for the bag in which the woman had placed the cheap flip flops.

Patricia blinked in surprise, but returned the smile. "You're welcome."

"Chop, chop," Tracey cut in, tugging Carlotta toward the escalator.

"How many people are supposed to be at this meeting?" she asked, climbing aboard.

"It depends on how many of Neiman's people will be there—this is the general manager's pet project."

"It's worthwhile," she murmured, wondering if Lindy Russell was the GM here. A pang barbed through her when she thought about Michael Lane, her former coworker and friend, who'd gone off the deep end and had been insti-tutionalized. But in this world was he still in the shoe department, breaking sales records? She was afraid to seek him out, to ask too many questions, still unsure of the "rules" of her wish fulfillment.

Tracey led the way through the administrative offices of the store—Carlotta had been in the GM's office a lot lately for various reprimands and other one-way discussions.

"And someone from the APD is supposed to be here," Tracey added as they approached the board room.

Carlotta's pulse shot up. "Really?"

"*Supposed* to be—no one would even return my call. You'd think with us arranging this benefit, the police people would be a tad more cooperative."

"I'm sure the police people have more pressing issues."

Tracey sniffed, then opened the door.

The first person Carlotta saw when she walked into the room was Jack Terry, standing apart from everyone else, holding up a wall. He wore slacks and a sport coat over a dress shirt and signature bad tie. From the expression on his face, either he didn't want to be there, or something sharp had found its way into his shoe… or both.

"Hello," she said. Her heart was stampeding her lungs.

He gave her a brazen scan, then suspicion colored his golden eyes. "Have we met before?"

A shiver traveled over her shoulders. "I don't think so. I'm Carlotta Wren."

Tracey bumped her, then gave her wedding ring a pointed look.

"Er, Ashford," she amended.

"Jack Terry," he ground out. "Why are you here?"

Carlotta's tongue stalled in her mouth.

Her friend gave her a strange look, then jumped in with a practiced intro-duction. "I'm Mrs. Dr. Tracey Tully Lowenstein. Carlotta and I are members of Deer Ferry Country Club. We're organizing the charity event to pay for the bulletproof vests."

Carlotta noticed that Jack's jaw hardened at the mention of the word "charity."

"It's our privilege to support the APD," she rushed to add. "We know the city budget doesn't cover all the equipment the department needs to do their jobs."

He grunted, then glanced at his watch, already bored.

Carlotta glanced over the handful of other people attending, recognizing her general manager Lindy Russell and a couple of directors. Lindy spoke to her as if they'd met before, but without the authority of being her superior at the store. Carlotta tingled with awareness to be speaking to people with whom she was so familiar, but who knew nothing of her except that she was a country-club do-gooder.

In the corner of the room sat three large boxes which, from the markings, contained the models of vests under consideration.

"Why don't we get started," Lindy suggested, gesturing toward the chairs around the table.

Carlotta found herself seated opposite of Jack, who seemed to be studying her again. She tried not to squirm, but it was bizarre to think about how much she and Jack had been through in the other world, yet here, he didn't even know her.

Tracey bumped her. Carlotta turned her head to see it wasn't just Jack who was looking at her—everyone in the room stared at her with an expectant air. Alarm shot through her when she realized that Lindy had turned the floor over to her.

"I..." Her throat convulsed. "I... confess I'm not prepared to speak to speak on the fly—"

"Which is why," Tracey cut in, "she brought notes."

Carlotta was utterly lost.

"On your iPad," Tracey muttered as she pulled out her own slick device.

"Oh... right," Carlotta said, remembering the gadget in her purse. "If you'll just give me a moment..." She removed the case from her bag, completely at a loss as to how to turn it on.

But Tracey must have picked up on her hesitancy. "I'll find our notes," she offered.

Carlotta gratefully handed over the device. To fill the awkward void, Carlotta manufactured a smile and said, "In the meantime, perhaps Detective Terry could tell us what the department is looking for in a bulletproof vest?"

Jack cocked an eyebrow, then spread his hands. "Uh... something that stops bullets?"

Laughter resounded around the room as a flush climbed her neck.

"Here we are," Tracey said, sliding Carlotta's iPad in front of her.

She looked down to see the notes she'd presumably written—a script for her and Tracey. To her horror, it appeared to be a monologue about the good deeds of the country club.

"I'll start," Tracey said magnanimously, then launched into reading the prepared statement about the police benefit that sounded incredibly self-congratulating.

Carlotta bit down on the inside of her cheek as Tracey droned on and Jack's eyes glazed over. The Neiman's employees looked equally bored.

"I think you'll agree that our efforts are very commendable," Tracey was saying, "and—"

"And," Carlotta cut in with a little laugh, "there's no need to be so formal. Why don't we just get down to the business of choosing a vest?"

"Good idea," Lindy agreed.

Tracey was momentarily thrown, then she recovered. "Okay."

"Let's see what we have here," Carlotta said, rising and moving toward the boxes.

"I'll read the descriptions," Tracey said, now back to form. She followed Carlotta and told her which box to open first.

Carlotta unwrapped and hauled out the first vest, surprised by its weight— at least thirty pounds. She awkwardly held it up for the others to see, focusing on Jack as Tracey read off a list of is features—material, color, style—as if she were emceeing a fashion show.

Jack pulled a hand over his mouth and Carlotta pinged with embarrassment.

"Put it on," Tracey whispered loudly.

Carlotta shook her head in protest, but Jack spoke up.

"By all means. It'll help me get a feel for how it'll work for our female officers. If fact, let me help you."

He stood and took the vest from her as if it weighed nothing, then unzipped it and held it behind her while she put her arms through the openings. He slowly zipped the vest and tightened the buckles, his sardonic gaze boring into hers throughout. Her body responded to his proximity, loosening here, contracting there. The electricity between them could've burned down Atlanta for a second time. It was as if they were the only two people in the room.

"What do you think of this one, Detective Terry?" Lindy interjected into the thick silence.

His lion gaze remained locked with Carlotta's. "I haven't made up my mind yet."

Her mouth opened to allow her breath to escape. She was sure everyone in the room could hear her heart pounding against the constraints of the Kevlar.

"Why don't we move on?" Tracey suggested, her voice high and artificially cheerful as she shot Carlotta a private, bewildered look.

Carlotta self-consciously unfastened the vest and shrugged out of it to try on the other two models, thinking to herself throughout how ironic the garments could stop bullets, but not protect her from Jack's animal magnetism.

While Tracey jauntily ticked off the features of the third vest, Jack's phone chimed. He pulled it out, glanced at the screen, then announced he needed to leave.

"But we're not finished," Tracey said, stopping short of stomping her foot.

"Any of the vests will be fine," Jack said, moving toward the door. "They all meet the department's requirements."

Tracey frowned. "That's all you can say? We went to a lot of trouble to choose these samples and to set up this meeting!"

"Then you two pick the one you think is the prettiest," he said, flicking his gaze over Carlotta. He gave the room a mock salute, and walked out.

Carlotta wanted to run after him, but she was weighted down by the bulletproof vest... oh, and her wedding ring.

CHAPTER SEVEN

"WHAT AN ASS that detective was," Tracey declared as she climbed into her white Escalade.

Carlotta smiled at the mall valet who held open the passenger door for her and slid into the seat. "He was probably just preoccupied," she offered, still shaken from the encounter.

Tracey put the SUV into gear and pulled away. "What was going on between you two?"

Carlotta tried on her innocent face. "What do you mean?"

"You know what I mean—I thought you and him were going to start humping on the table."

"That's ridiculous."

"I mean, I know you're concerned about Peter, but taking on a redneck lover won't help matters."

"I'm not taking on a lover," Carlotta said, irritated at Tracey's classification of Jack as being beneath them. "You misunderstood our... interaction."

"Uh-huh. Well, so tell me—did you find the pictures you were looking for?"

She reached into her purse to pull out the small yellow photo album. "You mean these photos from college graduation?"

"Yeah. Did you see anything to prove Angela and Peter have been seeing each other behind your back all these years?"

Carlotta inhaled sharply. "I... don't know."

"We'll look at them over lunch at the club," Tracey said with a wave. "I think we can both use a martini."

"Right," Carlotta murmured, mulling the new information. Since Peter had married Angela in her world, it made sense that they shared an attraction. She'd harbored guilt over Angela's death because she'd known that Peter's pining for her had affected the couple's marriage, and subsequently, Angela's behavior. Was the shoe now on the other foot? Maybe Peter was destined to yearn for a woman he couldn't have?

On the drive to the country club, Carlotta kept an eye on the digital clock on the high-tech dashboard. Time in this place seemed to be passing at a normal pace, at least.

Tracey noticed her checking the clock. "Are you on a schedule?" Then she laughed. "As if. When have either one of us been on a schedule? I guess we haven't done much with our pricey college degrees, have we?"

Carlotta smiled, but the comment left her feeling a little empty. She had no place to be at any time in particular? What did she *do* all day?

The Deer Ferry Country Club was much the same as it had always been—beautifully maintained on an exclusive plot of land, surrounded by a tall, ornate fence that served as a warning to riffraff to stay the hell out, thank you much very.

"Wow, look at the line," Tracey said when they pulled up to the valet stand. "I hope we don't have to wait for a table."

"There should be plenty of seating on the patio," Carlotta offered.

"Ack, and sit in the *sun*? My dermatologist would kill me."

"Oh… right."

Carlotta watched the beautiful people alight from their pricey vehicles, suddenly nervous for no good reason. She'd practically grown up at the club before her parents had fled town, and she'd been Peter's guest more than once recently. But at Peter's side, she'd known she was an outsider and was able to maintain her guard. How different would it be to walk in with people with whom she'd never broken ranks?

Better… or worse?

A few people said hello and waved as they entered. Carlotta responded in-kind to the faces she found vaguely familiar. And a few people who wouldn't speak to her when she'd accompanied Peter seemed exuberant enough now.

Tracey, of course, was part of that group.

Carlotta studied the blonde as they were seated near the restaurant entrance. Tracey had a Southern-belle stiffness about her, a product of being told at a young age to hold herself in restraint, and to never go out in public unless every hair was shellacked in place. The end result was a herd of clones in the restaurant wearing the same clothes and hairstyles, and speaking in the same nasal intonation. Carlotta realized with a start that most of these women wouldn't know how to conduct themselves in any other setting, and it was their unease with anyone or anything differ-ent that made them lash out. They cut down the unfamiliar before their own weaknesses and rigidity could be exposed. At that moment, she was very glad she'd had the freedom to do things these women would never experience.

Like help Coop to move bodies from crime scenes… and help Jack to solve a few real murder mysteries along the way.

A waitress stopped at their table and banged down water glasses. "Can I get you something from the bar?"

Carlotta looked up and did a double-take. "Hannah!"

Hannah Kizer was as tall and broad as ever, the culinary smock doing very little to hide her Gothic style and tattoos. Her shoulders went back. "How do you know my name?"

Mortification and sadness swept through Carlotta—of course Hannah didn't know her. She rushed to cover her gaffe. "I must have seen you here before."

"Nope," Hannah said evenly. "First day on the job."

"Well, Carlotta must know you from another restaurant," Tracey said sharply. "She didn't just pull your name out of thin air."

Hannah frowned at Tracey's tone. "Something from the bar?" she repeated through gritted teeth.

"Martini, extra dirty," Tracey chirped.

"And you?" Hannah asked Carlotta.

She hesitated, having seen Hannah lick her finger and use it to stir a drink she'd once served to Tracey, out of spite. "Do you have bottled beer?"

Carlotta could tell her worth had risen a notch with Hannah. "Coming right up."

When Hannah walked away, Tracey said, "You've never ordered beer before."

Carlotta shrugged. "It just sounded good today."

Tracey angled her head. "You're acting so strange... what are you taking?"

Did she normally take something? She'd seen a couple of prescription pill bottles in her purse. "Nothing."

"If you say so," her friend responded in a sing-songy voice. "Let's see those photos."

Carlotta pulled the small photo album from her bag and opened it, a little nervous about re-examining the photos for some indication of a relationship between Peter and Angela. Tracey pounced on them right away. "I remember thinking that Angela and Peter were pretty chummy at this party. Look at this one... everyone is looking at the camera except the two of them."

Peter and Angela were looking at each other.

"Same thing in this one," Tracey said a couple of pages later. "And this one."

Carlotta's stomach churned with anxiety. "But these pictures don't really prove anything."

"Only what you suspected—that this flirtation started in college. Add to that Peter's cagey behavior lately, the suspicious phone calls, and the rumors."

"Rumors?"

"You know—that Angela's been telling her friends that Peter isn't happy."

Carlotta bit her lip. "Does he seem unhappy to you?"

Tracey scoffed. "He seems as happy as any husband. They all think the grass is greener on the other side of the fence, when they should be watering their own damn grass." She glanced around. "Where's that martini?"

Carlotta eyed Tracey. The vehemence in her tone sounded like the voice of experience. "What's Freddy up to?" she asked delicately of Tracey's physician husband.

A vein popped out in Tracey's temple. "A two thousand dollar a week habit at the strip club."

Before Carlotta could react, Hannah reappeared with their drinks.

"Oh, thank God," Tracey said, taking the drink from Hannah's hand before she could set it on the table. "You might as well bring me another."

Hannah gave her a tight smile, then set a bottle of beer in front of Carlotta, along with a glass. "You didn't say, so I brought a local brew that's pretty tasty."

"Thank you," Carlotta said, and tried to telegraph to her friend that not only were they acquainted, but they'd had so many fun adventures together, from party crashing to body moving and even chasing down a few bad guys.

Hannah gave her a wary look. "Obviously, we've met before, but I'm sorry, I don't remember your name."

"Carlotta Wren." When Tracey bumped her, she added, "Ashford."

Carlotta could see the wheels turning in Hannah's head, could feel the connection and knew Hannah could feel it too. She felt guilty for putting her on the spot.

"We're ready to order," Tracey said in a tone meant to remind Hannah that she was there to serve them. Carlotta averted her gaze and took a drink of the good beer straight from the bottle.

"Sure thing," Hannah said. "What would you like?"

Tracey ordered a salad. Carlotta was famished, so she opted for the meatiest thing on the menu—a turkey burger.

"A beer and a burger?" Tracey asked when Hannah left. "If you weren't drinking, I'd ask if you were pregnant."

Carlotta nearly choked on her beer. Valerie had asked the same question. "No, I'm not pregnant."

"I don't blame you for putting the baby plans on hold until you figure out what's going on between Peter and Angela."

Baby plans? She lifted the bottle for another drink, but took only a sip, her hand snaking to her abdomen. What if she *was* pregnant in this life?

A well-preserved older woman walked up to the table and gave them both a wide, plastic smile. "Hello, girls."

A memory chord strummed in Carlotta's mind, but she couldn't place the woman.

"Hi, Bette," Tracey said.

Ah, Bette Noble, the woman who'd talked to her mother on the phone this morning.

"Hello, Bette," she added.

"How is the policemen's benefit coming along?"

The woman's gender reference rankled her. "The police *department* benefit is moving ahead."

"Yes," Tracey added. "We had a meeting this morning to choose which bulletproof vest to order."

"Let me know if I can help," the woman said in a superior voice. "My benefit last year was a record success. But don't feel pressured—no one expects you to top the money I raised."

Tracey had already emptied her martini glass. She opened her mouth to say something acidic, but Carlotta headed her off. "Absolutely, we'll let you know, Bette."

The woman smiled, then glanced at the photo album still lying open on the table. "By the way, Carlotta, I mentioned to Valerie that last week I saw Peter at a restaurant way up in Cumming."

"Yes," Carlotta murmured. "Peter has clients all over the metro area."

"It was a lady client," Bette said with a knowing smile. "In fact, it was *this* lady client." She pointed to the photo album, then tapped Angela's face. "Very pretty."

Carlotta's heart dropped, but she managed to conjure up a smile. "Yes… she's a very pretty friend of ours."

"That's good to know," Bette said, feigning relief. "I'd hate to be the source of bad news."

Tracey tipped her glass for the last few drops of vodka, leaving Carlotta to fend for herself.

"I'll tell Peter you said hello," Carlotta said with as much composure as she could muster. When the woman walked off, she muttered, "What a bitch," just as Hannah returned with Tracey's second martini. Hannah's mouth twitched and they shared a glance of solidarity.

Tracey took the second drink, then made a shooing motion to Hannah, bumping her empty glass in the process and sending it crashing to the floor. "Oops, sorry about that."

Hannah's cheek extended with the insertion of her tongue. "No problem. I'll get a broom… unless the one you rode in on is handy?"

Carlotta choked back a laugh as Tracey's expression went lethal. "You should really watch your mouth. It would be a shame if your first day on the job was also your last."

Hannah visibly bit her tongue, turned on her heel and stalked away.

"Tracey," Carlotta admonished.

"What? Are you forgetting the only reason she's here is because you got that last girl fired for putting too much lemon in your tea?"

Carlotta sat back, nonplused to hear that she was guilty of such petty behavior.

"Forget that," Tracey said with a wave. "Bette Noble is a bitch, but she did you a favor. Now you *know* Peter and Angela are having an affair."

Carlotta started to protest that a clandestine meal an hour outside the city didn't an affair make, but deep down, she knew there was no other explanation. The knowledge that Peter had taken vows with her, but had turned to another woman was like a knife to her heart. The fact that he'd just upgraded her engagement ring made it seem unlikely he was contemplating asking her for a divorce. Did that mean that he simply intended to keep Angela on the side?

"So," Tracey said, leaning in. "Are you going to do it?"

Carlotta was clueless as to what the woman was talking about, but the gleam in Tracey's eye concerned her. "Do what?"

Tracey glanced around to make sure no one else was listening. "Kill Angela."

CHAPTER EIGHT

IN THE SPAN OF TWO HEARTBEATS, Carlotta realized that Tracey was serious... dead serious. "What?" She tried to laugh.

"You said if you got proof Angela was messing around with Peter, you were going to kill her."

"I was joking... of course."

Tracey scoffed. "That list you showed me didn't look like a joke."

Carlotta's hand fisted in her lap. "List?"

"You know—how you were going to do it and get away with it."

"I..." She swallowed hard. "I would never do something like that, Tracey." Would she? Her relief that Angela Keener was still alive was somewhat mitigated by the fact that she herself was planning to murder the woman.

"Don't worry—your secret is safe with me," Tracey said in the sing-songy tone that was starting to tap dance on Carlotta's nerves. "But if you ever need to move a body, don't call me."

She frowned. "I won't."

Hannah appeared at that moment with a broom. Carlotta was so glad to see her, but she pinged with embarrassment as her friend knelt to deal with the broken glass.

A movement next to their table caught Carlotta's eye, then her heart vaulted to her throat. A man, dressed in black and wearing a ski mask, stood there with a pillow case in one hand, a gun in the other, marching the hostess, a security guard, and the valet captain in front of him, their hands in the air. "Ewywon, phut the phale ut!"

When hardly anyone in the noisy room noticed, he lifted the mask off his mouth. "I said, shut the hell up!"

That did it. Everyone in the room stopped, forks and glasses in mid-air, to gape. Someone screamed daintily.

The robber turned in a half-circle to address the diners in a thick drawl. "Nobody move. I'm going to need your wallets and your jewelry, just drop 'em in the bag. If anyone reaches for their cell phone to call the police, I'll put a hole in ya, got it?"

He started with their table. A wide-eyed Tracey dutifully dropped in her wallet and jewelry. Hannah scowled, but added numerous skull rings and snake bracelets. Carlotta reluctantly relinquished the rings Peter had given her only this morning, plus a watch, diamond stud earrings, then rummaged in her purse for her wallet.

He was pointing the gun directly at her with a shaking hand. At first she couldn't put her finger on what was wrong, then she realized she saw daylight through the round cylinders—the revolver was empty. Jack would be so proud of her for noticing.

She relaxed a bit… at least no one was going to get shot. She wasn't happy about being robbed, but she wasn't stupid enough to think she could overcome the man.

"Hurvy ut!" he yelled, pulling at his mask. She glared and dropped in the wallet. He moved on to the next table, waving the gun wildly to get the women to comply.

He was either high or nervous—or both. She realized he was having trouble seeing through his ill-fitting ski mask, and a plan started forming in her head as he jerkily made his rounds. The security guard was aged and unarmed—probably to appease the sensibilities of the mostly-female diners. Any doubts she had about intervening were put to rest when the robber used the revolver to backhand an elderly woman who didn't want to give up her wedding ring.

The brute simply couldn't get away.

She looked up and caught Hannah's eye, then tapped her temple. Hannah nodded that she understood that the man's field of vision was compromised.

Carlotta made a gun symbol with forefinger and thumb, then mouthed "no bullets." Hannah pursed her mouth, then nodded again.

The robber's bag was filling up—they only had a few seconds to stop him. Hannah held up the broom and gestured to the doorway. Carlotta nodded. Tucking behind tables, they positioned themselves on either side of the entrance with the broom between them.

The robber turned with an overflowing bag and lumbered toward the entrance, still pulling at his mask. He ran toward the door and didn't see the broom they raised to shin level as he went past them. The bag of stolen items went flying into the air and scattered spectacularly over the lobby of the restaurant. The robber hit the floor hard face-down… and his gun went off. His body jerked once, then he lay still.

Hannah looked up, her eyes wide. "I thought you said the gun was empty!"

Carlotta swallowed hard. "I thought it was!" She turned back to the dining room. "Someone call 911!"

They rushed to the still man's side and Hannah sank her fingers into the side of his neck. "No pulse. He's dead."

Before Carlotta could react, cheers went up behind them. She turned to see all the diners on their feet, yelling and applauding.

She and Hannah exchanged startled glances. They were heroes.

"Should we turn him over or something?" Hannah whispered. A red stain bled into the carpet beneath the man.

The wail of sirens approaching reached their ears.

"Maybe we should let the police handle it," Carlotta murmured.

"Do you think we're in trouble?"

Carlotta blinked. She and Hannah had been in countless scrapes together—including being arrested—and she'd never seen the woman flinch. She opened her mouth to say of course not when she saw Jack Terry barreling through the entrance, weapon drawn. She swallowed her words past a constricted throat.

They were, indeed, in heap big trouble.

He came up short next to the body and stared at her. "You!"

"Me," she confirmed with a shaky smile.

"Are you okay?" he asked.

She nodded.

Hannah raised her hand. "So am I, thanks for asking."

Jack grunted. "Where did the blood come from?"

"He fell on his gun," Carlotta said, "after we, um, tripped him."

"We think he's dead," Hannah offered.

Jack frowned. "Stand back."

She and Hannah retreated a few steps while Jack knelt and shook the robber. When he received no response, he gestured for a couple of uniformed officers who'd arrived to turn over the body while he kept his gun trained on the man. They flopped him over, but the robber remained lifeless. His black shirt was stained blacker with blood. The gun he'd wielded fell out of his hand onto the floor. One of the cops checked for a pulse, but shook his head.

Jack reholstered his weapon. "Call it in."

"And we need an ambulance for a woman he struck in the face," Carlotta said.

"On its way," Jack said. His scowl encompassed Carlotta and Hannah. "Would one of you like to tell me what the hell happened here?"

They told the story in halting tag-team fashion. After a minute, Jack massaged the bridge of his nose.

"What's your name again?"

"Carlotta Wren. Er—Ashford."

"Hannah Kizer, with a 'Z.'"

"And you two know each other?"

"Yes," Carlotta said, then checked herself. "I mean, we met today."

"Which one of you had the hare-brained idea to trip an armed man?"

At his sarcastic tone, Carlotta drew herself up. "It was a mutually agreed-upon plan."

He glared. "Well, you could've gotten yourselves or someone else shot."

"I thought the gun was unloaded," she declared hotly. "The cylinders were empty."

He cocked an eyebrow. "You know something about guns, do you?"

A flush climbed her neck. "A little."

"Well, apparently not enough," he said pointedly. "A man's *dead*."

Carlotta bit into her lip. "Are we in trouble?"

"Detective?" one of the uniforms said. "Will you take a look at this?"

They glanced over to see the man's mask had been removed to reveal a plump, grizzled face.

"Is this who I think it is?" the cop asked.

"Shit fire," Jack muttered, walking closer. "Duke Thornhouse."

"Looks like he's gone from robbing banks to robbing country clubs," the cop said. Then he grinned. "Guess these ladies did you a favor, Detective, bagging the man you've been chasing for years."

Carlotta's mouth opened with incredulity. The robber was a federal fugitive? She and Hannah exchanged private, wide-eyed glances, then Carlotta looked back to Jack. "You're welcome, Detective."

His jaw hardened, then he rebuked the grinning officer with a glare. "Take the statements of these two vigilantes," he barked. "And send a couple of uniforms into the restaurant to take down names and make sure everyone's stories add up."

Tracey had managed to slip into the lobby. "Hi, Detective Terry—remember me?"

He sighed, then nodded.

She beamed, then gestured at the items strewn on the floor. "Everyone is asking when we'll get our things back."

"At some future date. For now, everything has to be bagged as evidence."

She frowned. "We're talking about a lot of irreplaceable jewels, Detective." She lowered her voice and jerked her head toward the uniformed cops. "What if some of your men decide the temptation is just too much?"

He leaned in conspiratorially. "Then I guess we can buy our own bulletproof vests, and you're off the hook for the charity event."

Tracey's eyebrows came together.

Carlotta stepped up. "Detective Terry, the items weren't removed from the property—isn't there something you can do?" She wasn't above batting her eyelashes.

And he wasn't immune. He frowned. "Okay, but no one takes anything until everything has been catalogued." He pointed to Carlotta. "You, don't leave." He stalked away, his phone to his ear.

Tracey turned to Carlotta and handed her the Bottega Veneta pink leather hobo bag she was holding. "That man seems fixated on you."

"It's not me. Turns out the guy we took down is some kind of high-profile criminal."

Tracey's eyes went wide, then she crossed her arms. "Why didn't you ask me to help you instead of that waitress person?"

Hannah waved from a few feet away. "I'm right here, I can hear you."

"It just happened so fast," Carlotta improvised. "Why don't you help the officers inside the restaurant keep everyone calm?"

Tracey stomped off, and Hannah stepped closer. "Real treasure of a friend you got there."

"She's not so bad, she's just… sheltered."

"And you aren't?"

Carlotta gave Hannah a little smile. "Not as much as you'd think."

But Hannah's attention was snagged on something behind Carlotta. "Who is *that*?"

She turned to see a tall, lean man walk into the lobby and make his way over to Jack for a brief handshake. Cooper Craft. And in this place he wasn't a lowly body mover. The jacket he wore identified him as the Chief Medical Examiner.

CHAPTER NINE

COOPER CRAFT WAS ALL business as he and Jack surveyed the scene. His gaze stopped on Carlotta and her skin tingled.

"Do you know him?" Hannah asked.

"No."

"Well, he obviously knows you." Hannah tossed her black and white striped hair. "Here they come. Introduce us."

Apparently Hannah was crushing on Coop no matter which world they were in.

"This is Dr. Craft, Medical Examiner," Jack said. "He'd like to ask you a couple of questions."

Coop stuck out his hand to Carlotta. "Your name?"

"Carlotta Wren." Hannah bumped her. "Er... Ashford." She took his hand and warmth suffused her entire arm.

When he released her hand, he flexed his as if he'd had a similar reaction. "I'm sorry—have we met before?"

"I don't think so," she murmured.

"I'm Hannah Kizer." Hannah grabbed his hand for an enthusiastic pump. "I'm the unmarried one."

Coop gave her a little smile, but Carlotta noticed that his eyes were bloodshot. She wanted to give him the benefit of the doubt, that he was pulling a double shift and operating on little sleep, but she detected the scent of strong mouth wash. Was Coop drinking on the job? It was the reason he'd lost his job in the world she knew. Was he on the same path here?

"Detective Terry said the dead man tripped?" Coop asked.

"*We* tripped him," Hannah said, beaming. "With a broom."

He turned to Carlotta. "He fell on his weapon?"

"That's right. And it went off." She wet her lips. "I thought the revolver was empty, but obviously there was one round in the chamber."

He stared at her mouth. "Luckily the shot didn't fly wild. Did he move after he hit the floor?"

"No. He lay completely still."

"Did you notice anything else about him that might be important?"

"No," Hannah said.

"There was one thing," Carlotta offered. "I thought he seemed anxious or maybe high on something. Knowing now that he's a seasoned criminal, it makes more sense that he was on something versus simply being nervous."

He nodded. "Okay, thanks."

"You know, death has always fascinated me," Hannah said, leaning in and twirling her hair.

Coop's eyebrows rose. "You don't say?"

"Maybe I could get a tour of the morgue sometime?"

"Um, we do occasionally have educational tours."

Hannah beamed. "Sign me up."

"If we're done here," Jack cut in, "Dr. Craft needs to get back to the body."

"Right," Coop said. "Thank you, ladies." He nodded at Hannah, but his gaze lingered on Carlotta until Jack cleared his throat. The men walked away, with Hannah staring dreamily.

"I think I'm in lust."

Carlotta smiled. "I thought you were into married men."

"I am, but—" Hannah squinted. "Hey, how did you know that?"

Uh-oh. "I... guessed?"

Hannah frowned. "How about you don't make judgments based on my appearance, and I don't make judgments based on yours?"

Carlotta smiled. "Does that mean we can be friends?"

Hannah's frown deepened. "That remains to be seen."

Tracey re-emerged from the restaurant, clearly perturbed. "They're closing the restaurant."

"That's to be expected," Carlotta said.

"But I'm starving," Tracey snapped.

"The two martinis didn't fill you up?" Hannah asked dryly.

Tracey glared, then turned to Carlotta. "I thought we'd go to Spinnaker's. They have a nice lettuce wedge. And we can discuss your *list*."

Carlotta went cold. The last thing she wanted to do was discuss her alleged murder-plot list with Tracey. "You go ahead. The detective wants me to stick around."

Tracey looked slighted, then flounced away. Carlotta and Hannah waited and watched while the body was bagged and removed by a couple of guys wearing morgue jackets who, from the way they were handling the rather large body, were either new on the job or just didn't give a hoot.

Carlotta stepped forward. "You might want to use the gurney straps to secure the body."

The men looked at her and scoffed. "We got this, sweetheart," one of them said. But just as they reached the entrance, they hit a bump and the body rolled off, hitting the floor with a thud.

Coop charged toward them, and even though she couldn't hear what he said, it was clear from his body language that he was beyond upset with the men.

Hannah looked at her askew. "What do you know about moving bodies?"

"Nothing," Carlotta said in her most innocent voice.

Jack reappeared to confirm details about their earlier statements. "I'll need your home addresses and phone numbers for the report."

Carlotta balked. Where did she live? Her address would be on her driver's license, but she didn't have her wallet. When Hannah finished reciting her info, Jack turned to her.

"Phone number?"

She pulled out her cell phone and read off the number.

He wrote it down. "Address?"

"Um… I need my wallet."

Jack frowned. "You don't know your own address?"

"Uh… we had a recent zip code change," she improvised.

Jack waved over the officer who was emptying the pillow case and allowed Carlotta to retrieve her wallet. She flipped to her license that featured a photo of her sporting a shorter hairstyle, and read off the address—it was the same house that Peter lived in now... er, in the other place.

"And were any other items taken from you during the robbery?"

"Three sterling skull rings and two sterling snake bracelets," Hannah said. "I'm lucky he didn't take my nose ring."

Jack made a dubious note of it, then looked at Carlotta. "And you?"

"Diamond stud earrings and a sterling watch."

He glanced at her left hand. "I seem to recall you were wearing a wedding ring at the meeting this morning."

She swallowed. "Yes. A three-diamond Cartier engagement ring, and a matching gold wedding band."

He whistled low. "I take it your husband doesn't work for the city."

She didn't respond, but their gazes locked and she saw the same confusion in his gold-colored eyes as before... he felt their connection, but didn't understand why.

He directed them to a table where the jewelry had been sorted. A uniformed cop checked off the items they claimed. Carlotta silently slipped on her rings and studied them—was it her imagination, or did they feel even heavier?

"You act as if you've never seen those things before," Jack remarked.

She turned to find him studying her. "It's... hard to explain."

"Life's complicated, isn't it?"

There is was again, that tug between them that had erupted the second they'd first met in the police precinct... and still endured.

"Are you through with me?" Hannah asked Jack, breaking the moment.

"Yes."

Hannah looked at Carlotta. "I'd offer you a ride home, but I have another work gig to get to."

"I'll make sure Ms. Wren gets home," Jack said.

"Ashford," Hannah corrected.

"Right," he and Carlotta said in unison.

Hannah squinted back and forth between them, then lifted her hand in a wave to Carlotta. "Nice fighting crime with you. See you around the club."

She watched her friend give Coop an adoring glance as she passed him, then exit the club. Carlotta wondered if she and Hannah would ever be as good friend here as they were in the other place. It was, she supposed, a start.

Coop gave them a flat smile as he walked up. "I'm finished here unless you need something else, Jack."

"We're done. You driving straight home?" Jack gave him a pointed look that said he, too, had noticed Coop had been drinking.

Anger flashed in Coop's eyes, then he returned a curt nod. "Sure." He turned to Carlotta. "It was nice to meet you, Ms. Wren."

"Ashford," Jack corrected.

"Right," Coop said. His gaze lingered on her for a few seconds, then he turned and strode away, his long legs eating up the ground.

"Ready to go?" Jack asked her.

She nodded, suddenly nervous about being alone with him. When they exited, a TV reporter was jogging up the sidewalk. He shoved a microphone in Jack's face. "Detective, is it true that the notorious fugitive Duke Thornhouse was taken down in a gunfight during an attempted armed robbery?"

A muscle worked in Jack's jaw. "No comment."

Carlotta smothered a smile—they both knew it was only a matter of time before the fifty or so women dining in the club restaurant circulated the story about her and Hannah foiling the robber's escape.

He hustled Carlotta into a familiar dark sedan—how many times had she been in Jack's car? She settled into the seat, noticing it seemed much the same. From the empty coffee cup in the console, it appeared he was riding solo.

Jack slid into the driver's seat and clicked his seat belt into place.

"You don't have a partner?" she asked.

His jaw hardened. "My partner, Detective Marquez, is in the hospital recuperating from a gunshot received in the line of duty a few weeks ago."

Her pulse bumped. Detective Maria Marquez had perished in the other place, at the hands of a killer. "Is Maria going to be okay?"

That garnered her a sharp look. "How do you know my partner's first name?"

She caught herself. "I must've heard it on the news."

"She's going to be okay... but she has a long road back. What was your address again?"

She told him.

"Nice part of town," he offered.

"I suppose."

She studied his profile and allowed the electricity bouncing between them to charge the interior of the car. After a stretch of loaded silence, he looked over at her. "Are you sure we haven't met before?"

Her lungs squeezed. "Why do you ask?"

He shook his head. "I can't explain it. You just seem... familiar."

She couldn't resist toying with him. "How so?"

His gaze swept over her with the leisurely pace of a lover. "Maybe we should change the subject."

He looked back to the road and her mind clicked with the possibilities and fallout of telling Jack the truth about their "past." Would it send her hurtling back?

"Jack," she said carefully, "what would you think if I told you that you and I do know each other... in another life."

He looked at her sideways. "No offense, I don't believe in all that reincarnation jazz."

She smiled. "I'm not talking about reincarnation, I'm talking about a parallel life. And you and I do know each other in that life—intimately."

He snorted. "Sorry, I don't buy it."

Carlotta turned sideways in her seat. "What if I could prove it?"

"How?"

"I know things about you."

"Like?"

"Like that you're from Alabama."

He scoffed. "You can tell that from my accent."

"And when you're not on the job, you prefer jeans, black T-shirts, and western boots."

"Also not a stretch."

She wet her lips. "I knew your partner, Maria, in the place where I came from. She's beautiful, tall and willowy, with a mane of light brown hair." She had been jealous of the woman's interaction with Jack.

He blinked, then scoffed. "You could've seen her picture on the news."

"I didn't—I only arrived here today. In fact, I'm relieved to hear she's alive. She was killed in the place where I'm from, by her ex-husband."

He looked angry. "That's a terrible thing to say."

"It *was* terrible… he drowned her in her bathtub. His name was Garza."

Jack looked alarmed. "This isn't funny anymore. I don't know where you got personal details of Maria's life, but—"

"Is he stalking her here, too? He's a dangerous man, Jack. You have to stop him from hurting her—"

"That's enough," he cut in. "I'm starting to think you're the dangerous one."

"I'm not dangerous," she said calmly. "I'm from another place where our lives are taking different paths than the way things are here. In the other place, Tracey and I aren't best friends—Hannah and I are."

"The tattooed waitress?"

"Yes. She and I work for Coop, moving bodies."

"In this 'other place,' you and that Goth chick work for the morgue?" His disbelief was clear.

"Actually, Coop isn't the M.E.—he lost his job because of his drinking. He contracts to move bodies for the morgue, and he hired us to help him."

"You don't say?"

"And the fugitive you're after isn't the bank robber we stopped today, it's my father."

His eyebrow lifted. "Really?"

"Yeah… in the other place, he skipped bail on a white collar charge and was a fugitive for over ten years."

"Was?"

"Right. You caught him, um… yesterday."

Now he simply looked amused, as if she were a small child. "Good for me."

She swallowed hard. "Look, I know this is a lot to take in, but it's true. You and I and everyone else is living another life in the place where I came from."

He pursed his mouth. "And how did you get here?"

"In my car."

"You drove across the space-time continuum?"

A flush worked its way up her neck. "Not exactly. My car hasn't run in years. This morning I climbed into it and fell asleep, and when I climbed out… I was here."

He nodded solemnly. "I hate when that happens."

She turned back around in her seat. "Forget it. I wouldn't believe me either."

They drove in silence for a few moments. Carlotta stared out the window, looking for differences in this place, but the sky was the same color of blue, the grass just as green, the cars just as noisy. They entered the upscale community of Martinique Estates where Peter—and she—lived. The guard at the security gate called her Mrs. Ashford and waved them through.

"So where do *I* live?" Jack asked.

She looked over. "I'm sorry?"

"If you know so much about me, then where do I live?"

She pressed her lips together. "Actually, you've never told me. You're pretty closed-mouthed about your personal life."

"That's the first thing you've said that I can believe."

She angled her head. "But I know what you look like naked."

He squirmed in his seat. "That's impossible."

"You have a hairy chest."

"Okay, that's not a leap."

She leaned closer. "And your um, *pride* hangs left."

He looked up as if he had to think about it to confirm. "You had a fifty/fifty chance of getting that one."

"And you have a cute little mole on your right—"

"Whoa," he said, tapping the brake as if he could stop her from talking. "Lots of guys have moles under their shorts." He gave her a skeptical look. "If you know what my body looks like, where is my tattoo?"

"You don't have one." Unless he'd gotten one in this world?

But from his grunt she could tell she'd answered correctly. "Lucky guess," he said as he pulled the car into the driveway above the palatial home that sat below street level. He pulled the car to a stop and looked over at her. "But even if I could wrap my mind around what you're saying, there's a flaw in your story."

She frowned. "What's that?"

His bold gaze raked over her again, skating over erogenous zones he traveled many times. "No matter what universe I'm in, I don't mess around with married women."

Her body warmed under his scrutiny, strained toward his magnetic pull. "I know," she murmured. "But in the other world, I'm not married."

His mouth opened slightly and she could see the confusion again. He wanted to believe her, but he simply couldn't.

"Goodbye, Jack," she said with a little smile. "Take care of Maria."

She opened the door and stepped out onto the driveway, then gave a little wave. When his car pulled away, Jack was still staring at her. Her heart shook until his taillights disappeared. Then she turned back to the house where she lived.

With her husband.

CHAPTER TEN

AS CARLOTTA WALKED DOWN the driveway to the house she shared with Peter, dread billowed in her chest. She hadn't had time to think about her marriage and her life with Peter since he'd picked her up this morning, but she could no longer ignore it. Her husband had seemed cheerful enough earlier, if a little distant—had he been planning to meet Angela for a lunchtime tryst?

She checked her watch, then pulled out her phone to call Peter, but got his voice mail. She left him a breezy message to call her when he got a break. She ended the call and stowed the phone with worry gathering in her stomach. According to Tracey and Bette Noble, the Ashford marriage was in deep trouble. Perhaps the house they shared would shed more light on their marital issues.

It was, by all accounts, a lovely home, stately in intricate brick and wrought iron. A turnaround in front of the flaring steps circled a large fountain. The two-story entryway rose to glorious palladium windows. On the left was a four-car garage. To the right of the house, the brick extended to a pool and manmade waterfall—it seemed that she and Peter had built the identical home that he and Angela had built in the place she'd come from.

So perhaps it was Peter's home, and she and Angela were simply accessories?

She walked up to the front door, hoping one of the keys on her key ring would open the door. It did. But as soon as she crossed the threshold, the beeping of the security system sounded, warning her she had mere seconds to enter the personal code. She walked through the foyer to the keypad on the far wall and punched in the code she had used at Peter's house before... and it worked.

She stood in the silent house and turned a full circle, taking in the familiar layout of the first floor—great room, enormous kitchen, den, and sunroom—and the furnishings, which were also familiar. Apparently her and Angela's taste in decorating was as similar as their taste in men.

She wandered around other rooms of the first floor, filled with awe that she lived in all of this luxury, before climbing one of the two stairways that led to the second floor. The master bedroom was a suite, enormous, furnished with oversized dark furniture. The ceiling featured an elaborately trayed ceiling and skylight. The bedroom gave way to a sitting room with a massive fireplace, wet bar, and large-screen TV, and a verandah beyond sets of French doors. In another direction, a mirrored dressing room serviced large his and her closets.... although "her" closet was suspiciously sparse.

On a table sat a black and white photo of their wedding portrait. Carlotta picked it up, ran her fingers over their smiling faces, hoping she had been as happy that day as she looked. She was wearing Vera Wang, of course, a brilliant white halter dress with a full skirt, a long crystal-stuffed veil. Very nice. Peter was meticulous in a black tuxedo. They were as perfect as any picture in a bridal magazine. They had so much history and so much in common, by all rights, they should have a perfect marriage.

She turned over the frame and found what she was looking for—the date of their wedding. A few months after she would've graduated from college, so they'd been married for seven years.

The Seven Year Itch.

So had all of the love flowed out of their relationship, or had they simply grown bored with each other?

A thought struck her that had her returning the framed picture and crossing the hall. When she'd stayed with Peter during the time her life had been in danger, he'd put her in the guest room across from his. She'd realized sadly that Angela had slept in the room, that she and Peter had maintained separate bedrooms, at least during the end of their marriage before her life had been taken.

Carlotta opened the door and her heart sank to see signs that she occupied the lighter, airier room. On the night stand sat some of her favorite beauty products, and a desk in the corner was cluttered with things that probably belonged to her. She opened the door to the walk-in closet/dressing room and confirmed its vast space was jammed full of clothes and shoes in her style and size.

She walked in and ran her hands over the lavish outfits, pulling out a few gowns to hold in front of her in the three-way mirror, wondering to what event she'd worn the dresses. She and Peter must have an active social life.

Then she frowned at her reflection… at what point had she moved into her own bedroom? After rehanging the dresses, she made her way to the maple desk to glean more information about herself and the state of her marriage.

It was a beautiful, large piece of furniture, with numerous drawers and cubby holes. Her desk at home was crammed with overdue bills and correspondence. But she suspected Peter took care of their household bills… a fact that did not make her proud. Tracey's comment today about neither one of them having a schedule plucked at her. If she was a vapid do-little woman who served as a society placeholder, no wonder Peter was bored with her… she'd lived here for one day and was bored with herself.

Okay, so she was a bore… but was she a murderer? Had Tracey been telling the truth about a how-to list for offing Angela? If so, where did she keep it? She flipped through notepads and notebooks, scanning every piece of paper and scrap she found, alert for something incriminating. She found a pack of cigarettes and a lighter jammed into a cubbyhole, proof that she was still smoking on the sly. And to her delight she found her pink leather bound celebrity autograph book, the one that had been ruined from a dip in a swimming pool in her world. But this one was still intact. She flipped through, curious to see if she'd added any interesting autographs. To her amazement, she had autographs from big name rock stars and world-renowned entertainers, politicians who were household names, even a member of the royal family. And she had a feeling that she hadn't had to resort to crashing parties to get these high-profile signatures. Her lifestyle with Peter had obviously afforded her remarkable access.

A bottom desk drawer was locked, and she couldn't find the key in any of the little containers that held paperclips and other odd items. She checked her key ring and found a small key that fit. Her heartbeat sped up when she saw a stack of journals inside. She opened the first one and saw it contained entries for recent dates. Her skin tingled to see words in her own handwriting that she had no memory of writing. It seemed clear that she was concerned about her relationship with Peter, that he had become more distant of late, and that his normal easy-going patience had been replaced with a short fuse. She skimmed backward, going back four journals until she found the first hint of real problems in their marriage starting over a year ago. Peter had become consumed with work, leaving early and working late. It was he who had suggested that she'd be more comfortable in her own bedroom, so he wouldn't disturb her sleep with his erratic schedule.

Carlotta was gratified to see that his suggestion had hurt her deeply at the time—it indicated that she loved her husband and mourned what she saw as a loss of intimacy. She had moved across the hall to spite him—no surprise there—certain that he would miss her lying next to him and would insist that she move back.

And he had.

But she'd refused, still bruised from his rejection, determined to make him suffer. It was, apparently, the beginning of a standoff that had morphed into polite coolness as each of them had retreated to their own corners of the house. Still mired in gloom, she'd begun to suspect Peter was having an affair, although she hadn't been able to catch him in any lies. There had been times, however, when he'd ended phone calls abruptly when she entered the room, or excused himself to his home office and closed the door.

She had pondered the list of possible mistresses—women he worked with, clients, friends. But during an encounter with Angela Keener at a club function, she thought she'd detected something more than friendship emanating from the women when she looked at Peter. According to her diary entries, Angela was still single and working as a salesperson at a luxury car dealership, although racy rumors persisted about her personal life.

Carlotta bit down on the inside of her cheek. In the other place, Angela had led a double life: Mrs. Angela Ashford, well-heeled socialite and Kay, high class call girl. Had Angela's life followed a similar trajectory here?

She continued to read and gathered that in the last few weeks, she'd become convinced Peter was having an affair with Angela, and had begun to wonder how long it could've been going on. Carlotta's pulse climbed higher as the entries began to increase in intensity and anger toward Angela. She wrote that if she couldn't be Mrs. Peter Ashford, she didn't know what she'd do with her life. The last entry of four days ago read, *I don't like the thoughts that are going through my head.*

Carlotta set down the journal with a shaking hand, although she was relieved not to find any mention of a list. If she'd made a list, where would she have put it? Her mind went to the iPad in her purse. She retrieved it and exhaled—obviously she was more technically inclined in this world. But remembering how Tracey had turned on the device, she pressed the sleep/ wake button and was rewarded with a screen full of icons. Calling on her inner Wesley, she fumbled around and was able to find the file manager. The tablet must be new because there were very few files to scan, and none of them referred to a list. Still, she opened each document file to check.

She sat back, relieved.

Although the absence of a to-do murder list on her iPad might indicate that she knew enough not to commit such a list to a computer file.

She stood and glanced around the room, wondering where she might have hidden such a list. She checked the nightstand, her closet drawers, even under her mattress, but came up empty. Turning back to the desk, she looked for anything she might have placed a list inside—a book or a magazine. In the back of a drawer, her hand closed around a long, thin cardboard tube. When she pulled it out, she noticed the Vanderbilt University Commencement sticker and recalled Wesley's mocking question about whether the tube she'd received that day had contained an actual diploma.

Her throat convulsed as she popped off one end of the tube and removed the piece of rolled paper inside. Moisture gathered in her eyes as she read the letter informing her that unfortunately, she would not be receiving her diploma that day because she was deficient in the four classes listed.

She bit her lip—did anyone else know? Tracey's comment about neither one of them using their pricey college degrees came back to her. Obviously she thought Carlotta had graduated. Is that why she didn't work, because she couldn't rightfully list a college degree on her resume?

Her mind raced with helplessness over the embarrassment of riches she'd been given in this life, and how she'd squandered them. But as she churned over what to do and if she could do anything that would affect this life going forward, she noticed another piece of paper in the tube. Hoping it was documentation that she'd finished her degree, she pulled out the sheet of paper.

But at the sight of hand-written words on the paper, her hopes fell... and her lungs squeezed tightly. At the top of the sheet she'd written the words *How to Kill a Mistress*.

CHAPTER ELEVEN

CARLOTTA FOUGHT TO BREATHE as she scanned the list she'd made to off the person she suspected was having an affair with Peter.

Learn her schedule. Set up an alibi. Make it look like an accident. Beneath the bulleted points were details about trailing the person and using the upcoming police benefit as a cover when the "deed" happened. The notes were cryptic but she got the feeling she was planning some kind of carjacking or ambush... and that she intended to carry it out with a gun or a knife, although thank goodness it appeared that she hadn't yet procured a weapon. She'd written notes to herself including "stay off the Internet when doing research." Carlotta pursed her mouth, wondering why she hadn't reminded herself not to share the existence of the list with a frenemy.

She was an idiot. A murderess and an idiot.

Her mind replayed a conversation she'd once had with Jack where he'd commented that everyone had the capacity for murder. Apparently, he was right.

She hugged herself, horrified to learn that she could go to such a dark place. Even if Angela was sleeping with Peter, she didn't deserve to die for it. Peter was the one who'd taken vows with her, not Angela. And if he wanted to be with Angela, Carlotta would give him his freedom.

Meanwhile, she had to get rid of this incriminating list.

She returned to the desk and retrieved the cigarette lighter, panicked now that she would somehow be sucked back through the time vortex before she could undo this horrible plan. She carried the paper into the spa-sized bathroom and held it over the commode while she set fire to the corner. Flames blackened, then dissolved the paper as they climbed upward. She held on to the paper until the last possible moment, then dropped it into the toilet bowl and flushed it away, heaving a sigh of relief.

But she was still trembling as she backtracked to the bedroom and sat down at her desk. She selected a pen, then opened the journal and began with *Dear Carlotta, this is a letter from yourself, from another place...*

She went on to describe how she'd wound up walking in her designer shoes, how she'd always wondered what her life would've been like if their parents hadn't abandoned her and Wesley and she'd been allowed to follow the path set for her early on.

But I'm disappointed to learn that my (your) life is empty and without purpose, that you haven't fostered your marriage, and worse, that you are on the verge of doing something evil. I destroyed the list. Everything I've been through has shown me how precious life is. If you love Peter, rededicate yourself to your marriage. If it turns out that he's in love with someone else, let him go. I'm proof that you are more than Mr. Peter Ashford, but only if you want to be. Finish your college degree, and find something useful and interesting to do with your time besides lunch at the club. You are more capable than you give yourself credit for. Expand your circle of friends to include people from all walks of life. Take more of an interest in Wesley and keep an eye on him—you can be a great source of strength for each other.

Oh, and keep the Miata.

She had just closed the journal and returned it to the locked drawer when the thought hit her like a lightning bolt that she'd been expecting at some point to be transported back to the place she'd come from... but what if she'd been dropped here to stay? What if after years of wishing her life had been different, she'd been granted her wish... and it was permanent?

While her mind reeled with the new revelation, the phone in her purse rang. She pulled it out, nervous about talking to anyone, but smiled when she saw Peter's name on the screen. She connected the call. "Hello."

"Carly?" His voice was agitated. "I just heard about the robbery at the club. Are you okay?"

"I'm fine."

His breath whooshed out. "Oh, thank God. I've died a thousand deaths."

Her heart filled up to hear the sincere concern in his voice. This man loved her... didn't he?

"I heard that you had something to do with the robber being captured? Is that true?"

"Yes."

"But Carly... that's so dangerous! That doesn't sound like something you'd do at all."

"I guess I'm braver than anyone gives me credit for," she said lightly.

"I guess so," he conceded. "The important thing is you're safe."

"I am. How did you hear about the robbery?"

"I, uh... actually, Angela told me."

Her pulse blipped. "You saw Angela today?"

"Um... we had coffee. I'd just gotten back to my office and picked up your voice message when she called to tell me that her mother had told her."

"Oh." So he'd taken Angela's call before returning hers.

"Where are you?"

"I'm home," she said cheerfully, then held up her hand. "Sitting here admiring my gorgeous new ring."

He gave a little laugh. "I'm so glad you like it."

"I don't like it... I love it."

Another pleased laugh sounded. "Good." After a few seconds' hesitation, he added, "Carly... we need to talk."

Her heart squeezed. "I'd like that. When?"

"Tonight, after your father's party?"

"Okay."

"I was planning to come back and pick you up, but I'm afraid I'm going to be stuck in a meeting all afternoon."

"Don't worry about it—I'll get Wes to give me a ride."

"Sounds good. I'll let your dad know you're okay. See you soon?"

"See you soon," she managed past a narrowed airway. She disconnected the call, besieged by the feeling that she was too late to save her marriage. The irony of arriving just in time for her life to fall apart seemed unbearably cruel.

Her phone vibrated in her hand. It was her mother. She still couldn't wrap her mind around the fact that she could talk to her mother on the phone. She connected the call.

"Hello?"

"Carlotta? Are you okay? Bette Noble just called me with the most absurd story!"

"The club was robbed," Carlotta confirmed. "But I'm fine."

"Thank goodness. Oh, how terrifying! But Bette said you killed the robber—is that true?"

"No," Carlotta said firmly, wondering how many versions of the story were going around. "He fell on his gun and shot himself. Everyone else is fine."

"Unbelievable. What is this world coming to?"

She bit her tongue to keep from commenting that the Valerie she knew had walked outside the law herself. "Is Wes around? I'd like to talk to him."

"He's in his room. Why don't you call him on his cell? That would be easier than me trying to get him to open the door."

"You could take the door off the hinges," Carlotta suggested mildly.

"I couldn't do that," Valerie said, her voice shocked. Then she added, "Could I?"

"Yes. You're the parent." The words came out more vehemently than she'd meant.

"I know that." Valerie sounded injured. "I just don't feel strong enough to deal with him."

"Then stop drinking." There... she'd said it.

After a shocked silence, her mother said, "You're way out of line."

"I'm your daughter, and I love you."

"And you have your life so together that you can criticize other people?"

Carlotta swallowed. "No. But I'm working on getting my life together."

After a lengthy silence, Valerie said, "Will I see you at your father's party?"

Deflect, ignore, postpone.

"Yes, I'll be there," Carlotta said softly. She disconnected the call with a sigh, then retrieved Wes's number on her phone. He answered on the third ring. Loud music thumped in the background.

"Somebody dead?"

She blinked. "No."

"Can't remember the last time you called is all."

She felt contrite. "I'm sorry, I've been a little self-absorbed lately. I was wondering if I could get a ride with you to Dad's work party."

He scoffed. "I'm not going to that snooze fest."

"I think you should, it's a big deal."

"No way—I have plans."

Carlotta counted to three. "Fine. Can you at least give me a ride?"

"Why should I?"

"Because I've had a rough day. I was at the club today when it was robbed at gunpoint."

"No shit?"

"In fact, I took down the perp. He was a federal fugitive."

"Now I *know* you're jerking my chain."

"Check the Internet. And if you want details, be here in thirty minutes. Wear a nice jacket." She hung up before he could respond, but she knew she'd piqued his interest.

She didn't have time to shower and she balked at the thought of changing into something from the vast closet—she felt attached to the clothes she'd arrived in, and the items she'd bought at Neiman's made the outfit dressy enough for an impromptu cocktail party. She did, however, make good use of the impressive and luxurious supply of toiletries and makeup to freshen up her face and smooth her hair.

She paused and studied her reflection in the vanity mirror, wondering about the woman who had sat here yesterday, and if she was beyond salvaging. She wouldn't wish the heartache and anguish she herself had experienced on anyone, but the ordeal had equipped her for the realities of life far better than someone allowed to grow up in the Buckhead bubble of entitlement.

The sound of a horn honking turned her head. That would be Wes, brimming with hostility... and curiosity. She grabbed her purse and jogged down the stairs, wondering if this grand place would remain her home.

She supposed it hinged on what Peter had to say... and her response.

After resetting the security alarm, she walked out the front door and waved at Wes, gawking over the enormous sport utility vehicle. "You drive a Humvee?"

He frowned. "Since my sixteenth birthday. Where the hell have you been?"

"Obviously not paying attention," she murmured as she climbed up into the passenger seat of the massive vehicle and slammed the door behind her. She was glad to see that he had at least worn a sport coat over his jeans and T-shirt. It mean that some part of him wanted to please her.

"Valerie said the party doesn't start until five-thirty. Why did you have me come so early?"

"I want to buy a congratulatory gift for Dad."

He rolled his eyes. "You don't expect me to take you shopping?"

"Just one place—Moody's cigar shop downtown."

He pursed his mouth. "Okay. Are you going to tell me what happened at the club? Mom said you're some kind of hero." He almost smiled.

"I'll tell you on the way."

He drove, rapt as she retold the story.

"Wow, Sis, I didn't know you had it in you?"

She turned her head. "You didn't?"

He shifted in his seat. "I mean... I always thought you were stronger than anyone gave you credit for."

For a few seconds, he looked like the Wesley she knew—sweet and vulnerable. "That goes for you, too."

He didn't respond for a long time, weaving in and out of traffic. Then he said, "We're different than Randolph and Valerie... aren't we?" He looked at her with almost pleading eyes.

She nodded and gave him a little smile. "If we want to be. I'm sorry I've been absent lately. But I want that to change... I'd like for us to spend more time together."

He was quiet, but she took the fact that he didn't object as a positive sign.

"Is this the place?" he asked, pointing.

She looked out the window and smiled at the familiar exterior of the beautifully restored building. "This is Moody's."

He pulled the Humvee into a parking place and turned off the engine. "No offense, but it doesn't look like a place you'd hang out."

She grinned. "Precisely."

She opened the door and jumped down, wondering if June Moody still owned and ran the place. The exterior of the cigar bar looked much the same as she remembered. Wesley surprised her by stepping up and opening the door. She crossed the threshold, much relieved to see the black horseshoe bar and art deco interior that she knew so well.

It was still early for the happy hour crowd that would pack the martini bar on the second floor.... but apparently the lone figure sitting at the bar had gotten a head start.

Cooper Craft.

CHAPTER TWELVE

COOPER TURNED HIS HEAD when they walked in. He was mid-drink. He held the liquid in his mouth as he perused Carlotta up and down, then he swallowed. "Hi... again."

"Hello," she said with a nod.

He set down his drink and stood. He was no longer wearing the jacket that identified him as the Chief Medical Examiner, just slacks and a long-sleeve shirt with the cuffs rolled up. "Carlotta, isn't it?"

"Yes. And you're Dr. Craft."

"Coop," he corrected, staring at her as if she were an apparition.

"And I'm Wesley, her brother," Wes said with a mock salute.

Coop's gaze cut to him, then he extended his hand. "How are you, man?"

Wesley straightened and accepted his firm handshake with a solemnity that made Carlotta wonder if any adult male had ever treated Wesley like an equal.

"I thought you told Detective Terry you were going straight home," Carlotta said mildly.

Coop had the grace to blush. "I live nearby."

"How do you two know each other?" Wes asked.

"Coop is the Medical Examiner," Carlotta offered. "He was on the, um, crime scene today."

"You're the Coroner?" Wes asked, impressed.

Coop looked around, then nodded in a way that said he was trying to be incognito at the moment.

"So you bagged the guy my sister offed?"

Carlotta frowned. "He offed himself."

"I'll make the final determination," Coop said, then his eyes twinkled. "But the evidence at the scene suggests that your sister is telling the truth."

"You have a cool job," Wes said.

"It's cool some of the time," Coop admitted. "But not everyone can work with stiffs all day. Buy you a beer?"

"Sure," Wes said happily.

"No," Carlotta cut in, then added to Coop. "He's not old enough to drink."

Wesley frowned. "I drink all the time."

"Well, you shouldn't," Coop said. "What brings you into Moody's?"

Carlotta smiled. "A congratulatory gift for our father."

"What's the occasion?"

"A promotion."

"Ah… nice."

At the sound of footsteps on the stairs, Carlotta glanced up to see June Moody descending gracefully. The woman was in her mid-fifties and dressed with the elegance of a Hepburn.

"Hi, June," Carlotta said, so pleased to see her.

June returned the smile. "Hello. Nice to see you."

Carlotta realized with a jolt that the woman didn't recognize her, but was being cordial, just as she would be to any customer.

"May I help you?" she offered.

Carlotta turned to Wesley. "Would you find something nice for Randolph?"

"Me? I don't know anything about cigars."

June winked and gestured with a manicured hand. "Come… I'll teach you."

Carlotta marveled as the petulant, foul-mouthed teenager with the attitude morphed into a polite young man. His eagerness tugged on her heart—he was starved for adult attention.

When they walked away, Coop turned to her. "Shall we sit?"

She agreed and lowered herself to the stool next to him.

"So," he said, "we meet again."

"So it would seem." She could tell from the slight glaze of his eyes that he was buzzed.

His mouth opened slightly. "Are you sure we've never met before today?"

"I guess it's possible," she said carefully.

He glanced at her wedding ring. "I'm not coming on to you… I just can't shake this feeling of déjà vu."

"I feel it, too," she said. "Actually, I know someone very much like you."

He gave a little laugh. "Poor fellow."

"He's been through some rough spots," she admitted. "He had a job very similar to the one you have now." She nodded to his glass. "But he made a terrible mistake and lost everything."

Coop wet his lips. "How's he doing now?"

"He's resilient, but he'd give anything to hit the rewind button."

Coop nodded slowly, but remained silent. He looked at his drink glass, then back to her. "Why do I have the feeling that you're some kind of messenger?"

She smiled. "Because… I am."

He arched an eyebrow and scanned her face, then he scoffed. "I must be loaded."

"Maybe," she conceded. "But when you sober up, I hope you'll remember this conversation."

He pursed his mouth. "I won't forget you, that's for sure."

"Hey, Sis," Wes said, striding up. "What do you think about this one?" He held a fat brown cigar reverently. "June says it's really rare and it smells great. Do you think Dad will like it?"

Carlotta nodded. "Looks good to me. Can you wrap it?" she asked June.

June smiled. "I can put it in a cardboard tube and add a red bow."

"Perfect." She looked at Wes. "Keep Dr. Craft company while I pay for the cigar?"

She left the men and followed June to the cash register. June busied herself with the sale, but glanced up. "I'm sorry, I can't place your name."

"Carlotta Wren… er, Ashford."

"You know Coop?"

"Actually, we met earlier today."

"Really? Funny, you two seem more familiar with each other."

Carlotta smiled. "I guess it's just like that for some people."

June nodded in concession.

"Do you mind if I ask you an odd question?" Carlotta said.

"Not at all."

"Has your life turned out the way you planned?"

June hesitated. "No. But then has anyone's?"

"You don't believe in destiny?"

The woman laughed lightly. "I think destiny is overrated. People get too caught up in what they think they're supposed to do or be. Instead of living life, they wind up chasing some optimum version of it, and missing out on all the good everyday stuff."

Carlotta pondered the woman's words. "In other words, there's no one best path."

"Right. At least that's what I think." She nodded to Carlotta's hand. "I see you're married."

Carlotta rummaged in her purse to find her wallet. "Yes."

"And is he a good man?"

Carlotta pulled out a credit card and handed it over. "Yes."

June took the card. "Then aren't you a lucky one?"

Carlotta nodded thoughtfully, then glanced over at Coop. He and Wesley were deep in guy-talk about cars and engines. She had never seen Wes more animated. Anger toward her parents shot through her—they hadn't abandoned her and Wes, yet they weren't present in their children's lives. Was this way really any better?

She thanked June for the cigar, and slipped it into her shirt pocket for safekeeping. When she walked over to the men, they were still talking automotive.

"Did you tell Wes about your '72 Corvette?" she asked Coop.

He blinked. "How did you know I have a 'Vette?"

"You must've mentioned it," she said softly. "How else would I know?"

He studied her solemnly, then paled and pushed his half-full drink away.

"We should get going," she said to Wes.

Wes looked disappointed, but nodded. "Nice talking to you," he offered to Coop.

Coop pulled out his wallet and fished out a business card. "Don't know if you're interested in medicine or lab work, but we can always use a bright intern at the morgue."

Wes took the card, but made a face. "My grades aren't so good."

"Then you should do something about that," Coop said, standing and pushing off his stool.

Carlotta wanted to kiss him. A few words from him meant more to Wes than anything she or their parents could possibly say. She mouthed "thank you," to the man, and, after a few seconds of silent communing with their eyes, he mouthed the words back.

"See you around," Wes said as they moved toward the door.

"I hope so," Coop said.

Carlotta gave him one last look, then waved to June and walked outside.

"Cool guy," Wes offered as they climbed into the Humvee.

"I think he liked you, too," Carlotta offered, buckling her seat belt.

Wes put the business card in his jacket pocket and started the engine. "This has been the weirdest day."

"Why do you say that?" she asked lightly.

"I don't know," he said. "I just feel... happy." He blushed furiously. "How lame is that?"

"It's not lame at all," she said with a wink. "I know exactly what you mean."

On the drive back to the Buckhead office building where Mashburn, Tully & Wren Investments was located, she quizzed him about school, about his grades, and if he'd thought about his future.

It was clear that while he was intrigued to think that he had the smarts to do something with his life, he still clung to his dumb jock identity.

"I don't want to turn into Randolph," he said as he pulled into a parking garage for the Buckhead financial district. "A slave to some stinking shirt-and-tie job."

"So instead you're going to be a slave to a drug habit?" she asked. "And live with Mom and Dad forever?"

He scowled. "It's not like I'm an addict."

"Prove it. Get your life together and get out on your own."

He gave a little laugh as he pulled into a parking place. "Yeah, because you're so independent."

"Touché." She angled her head. "Pact?"

Wes looked suspicious. "What do you mean?"

"Let's both *do* something with our lives."

"Like what?"

"Finish our education, for one. And maybe the morgue could use two interns."

His eyes bulged. "You? Working at the morgue?"

She shrugged. "Sounds intriguing, doesn't it?"

He pursed his mouth and nodded. "More interesting than school... and being in that house with the Stepfords."

"So we have a deal? We're both going to get our lives together?"

He looked uncomfortable. "So why the big change in you all of a sudden?"

"Chalk it up to my close call today at the club. When someone has a gun pointed at you, you tend to evaluate your life."

He smirked. "I guess you're right." But he still looked unconvinced... wary.

"Wes, we have to stick together, keep each other honest, okay? I need your help."

"Okay... I'm in."

She grinned. "Good. Now let's go in and play nice."

He grimaced. "I'd rather be somewhere else."

Nursing a pang for her old life, Carlotta was starting to fear she'd been plopped into this unpredictable place for good. "I know exactly what you mean."

CHAPTER THIRTEEN

THE ONLY THING DIFFERENT about the offices of Mashburn, Tully & Wren Investments since the last time Carlotta had been there to visit Peter was the fact that her father's name in gilt letters hadn't been scraped off the door.

Carlotta was happy to see Quinten Gallagher was still receptionist at the firm, but she was surprised by the frosty greeting.

"Welcome, Mrs. Ashford," he said with thinly veiled contempt, then his gaze bounced to Wes with equal disdain. "Mr. Wren."

She murmured a response, wondering how nasty she had been to this man in the past.

"Our new intern Meg will show you to the room where the party is being held."

The attractive young dishwater-blonde was familiar to Carlotta, but it took her a minute to recognize her from her previous world as Meg Vincent, the girl who worked with Wesley in the city office where he performed his community service work—and on whom he had a huge crush.

And from the way he was looking at her now, he was just as smitten.

"I'm Wesley Wren," he announced, his chest puffed out.

Meg sniffed and turned for him to follow her. Carlotta bit back a smile. It seemed the girl was as immune to Wes's charms as ever.

"I'll catch up," Carlotta said, then turned back to Quinten. "I'm sorry we haven't gotten to know each other. Would you like to have lunch sometime?"

He thawed right before her eyes. "Sure. That would be... nice."

"Great," she said, then turned and followed Wes and Meg to a noisy conference room where people mingled around a table that held a cake heralding "Congratulations."

She stiffened when she saw Walt Tully, Randolph's partner and Tracey's father, also her godfather, standing next to Randolph. Walt had led the charge against her father and had abandoned his godchildren during their time of need. She had to hide her loathing when the man smiled his waxy smile and gave her a one-armed hug.

"There's the woman of the hour," Walt boomed. "Tracey said you were quite the hero today at the club."

"I wouldn't go that far," Carlotta said, trying not to recoil.

"What were you thinking?" Randolph said, enveloping her in an embrace.

The feel of him, the smell of him made tears well in her eyes. She held on, prolonging the hug. He squeezed her hard, then pulled back. "You okay?"

She nodded, fine with him thinking she was overcome by what had happened at the club versus being overwhelmed hugging a father for which she'd yearned for more than a decade. "Congratulations. I'm so proud of you."

He smiled wide and squeezed her again. "I'm proud of you, too. You were brave today."

"Or foolish," Valerie said, her voice chiding. But when Randolph released her, she hugged Carlotta close and hard. "What would I do without you?" she whispered in Carlotta's ear.

Carlotta closed her eyes. She'd hungered to know whether her mother had regretted leaving, if she'd missed her daughter while she was in exile... it appeared she had.

When Valerie pulled back, Carlotta was happy to see Valerie's dark eyes were clear and lucid. "I talked to your father about Wesley," she said, for their ears only. "We're both going to keep closer tabs on him." She stroked Carlotta's hand. "I was wrong before... you'd make a wonderful mother."

Carlotta's throat was so clogged with emotion, she could only nod.

"Now... where is that handsome husband of yours?"

Carlotta glanced around the crowded room, but didn't see Peter. "Probably in his office—I'll find him."

She left the room feeling as if she were floating, buoyed by the sense that her family was going to be all right. It was the happiest she'd been since before her father had been indicted and their world had imploded.

When she reached Peter's office, the door was ajar. She opened it and saw he was on the phone, leaning against his desk, his back to her.

She walked closer, her ears piqued when she realized he was speaking to someone in an intimate voice, and in low tones. Snatches of the conversation drifted to her.

"… not ready to tell can't do this, Angela…. have to come clean… not good for either one of us."

Carlotta must have gasped or either he sensed her presence because he turned. When he saw Carlotta, he paled. "I'll call you back," he said into the phone, then set it down.

She crossed her arms, fighting back tears. "You're missing my father's party so you can have a private conversation with Angela Keener?"

He sighed. "How much did you hear?"

"Enough," she said evenly.

He held up his hands. "Carly, it's not what you think."

"Then clear it up for me." She was shaking now. "Explain why you've been seen having lunch with her in out of the way places."

He massaged the bridge of his nose, then walked closer. "Angela is involved in something illegal, and she came to me for advice."

She stopped, wanting to believe him. "What's she involved in?"

He averted his eyes. "I promised I wouldn't say—"

"What about your promise to me?"

He sighed again. "You're right. Okay… she's a call girl."

Surprise shot through her. "What?"

"I know, I couldn't believe it either when she told me. She got behind on her bills, and a girlfriend told her she could make some quick money. But now that she's in, the people she works for won't let her out."

Carlotta frowned. "Why did she come to you?"

He shrugged. "We grew up together, our families know each other. She trusts me. I'm trying to talk her into going to the district attorney's office with names to try to save herself."

She lifted her chin. "Is that all that's going on between you?"

Disbelief flashed over his face, then he clasped her arms. "Carly, I'm sorry I've been secretive—I should've told you what was going on. But Angie is just a friend, that's all. I couldn't possibly be attracted to another woman."

He kissed her earnestly, and she felt his desperation to prove his love for her. She opened her mouth and welcomed his tongue, swept up in his fervor. When they were young, Peter had been an ardent lover, but as a man, stress and emotional baggage had hampered his libido. They hadn't been able to consummate their reunion in the place she'd come from, but the insistent erection now pressed against her stomach was reminiscent of their early lovemaking. When he released her to close and lock his office door, she didn't stop him.

He walked her back into his desk. "I was scared to death when I heard about the robbery at the club. I want you…. I want to hold my wife."

"I want you, too," she whispered, fumbling with his belt and zipper.

He lifted her onto the desk and she toed off her sandals. They hit the floor with a thud as Peter shucked off her thin stretchy black pants and cotton undies. The edge of the desk cut into her bare thighs, but she didn't care. When she released his shaft into her hands, he sucked in a breath. He held her around the waist and she guided him home, breathless when he thrust into her. This was the lover she remembered, passionate and spontaneous, making her feel as if she was the most desirable woman in the world.

They fell into a frantic rhythm. He kissed her hard and deep, thumbing her sensitive center until she shook in his arms. She hadn't yet recovered when he took his own release, groaning against her neck. At that moment she felt awash with love and utterly safe in his embrace. It was a sensation she hadn't felt in years, and she reveled in it.

He lifted his head and gave her a lopsided grin. "Do you think they're missing us at the party?"

She laughed. "Probably not, but we should get back."

They disentangled and straightened their clothes. Carlotta slipped her feet back into her sandals when she saw a gold-colored gift box on the desk. "Did you get Daddy a gift?"

He grimaced. "No. You're determined to ruin the surprise."

"What surprise?"

"I lied. The fact that Angie is in trouble isn't the only reason I've been seeing her."

Unease niggled at her until he opened the box and held up a Mercedes car key.

"I bought you a new car."

She remembered reading in her journal that Angela worked at a luxury car dealership. She gasped with delight, and lifted on her toes to kiss him. "You're so good to me."

"I thought it was high time my wife had a grown-up car."

It was only then that panic blipped in her chest. "Where's my Miata?"

He smiled. "In a better place."

She frowned. "What does that mean?"

"A car broker gave me a great price for it—"

"You *sold* my car?"

His expression was a mask of patience. "I knew you wouldn't out of sentimentality. But come on, Carly, you need something more reliable to drive."

"You mean something more *appropriate* to drive, don't you? My father gave me that car—it means a lot to me."

He sighed. "If Randolph's feelings are hurt, you can blame it on me."

She was seething now. "It wasn't your decision to make!"

His mouth flattened. "It's already done—the guy towed it from your parents' garage this afternoon."

Her mind raced with the increasingly real possibility that without her Miata, she was stuck here. Her heart sprinted in her chest. She pointed to the phone on his desk. "Call the guy. Buy it back."

He paled. "I can't do that."

"Why not?"

"Because the guy doesn't have a car lot. He has a chop shop—"

"A chop shop!"

"He said the parts were in high demand," Peter said, back-pedaling now. "It's why he was able to pay so much for it."

She picked up a memo pad with a shaking hand. "Write down the address."

"Carly—"

"Write it down!"

He scribbled on the pad, then tore off the top sheet and handed it to her with a pained expression. "I was only trying to take care of you."

She gave him a sad smile. "I know, Peter. And I'm sorry I put you in that position."

She left his office and strode back to the conference room. Walt Tully was making a toast to her father. She picked up a glass of champagne from a tray and drank to Randolph. Her heart swelled with pride—this was the father she missed, the successful, honorable man. She felt torn... if she went back, she wouldn't get to spend time with this man. The father she'd go back to was a federal fugitive, sitting in jail. Father-daughter time in the other place would consist of timed conversations through Plexiglass with Randolph wearing a prison jumpsuit.

But for better or worse, it was the life she knew... and the one she wanted to return to, if she could.

She gave her parents one last look to drink them in, then threaded her way through the crowd to tap Wesley on the shoulder. "Can you take me somewhere?"

He glanced at Meg standing a few feet away, studiously ignoring him. "Now?"

"Now."

"You drag me here and now you want to leave?"

She pulled him toward the door. "It's important."

He gave Meg a wistful look. "Okay, okay. Where's the fire?"

"It's not a fire," she said, jogging toward the elevator. "Peter sold my convertible."

Wes stopped. "So?"

"So," she said, tugging on his arm. "I have to get it back."

"This very minute?"

"This very minute it could be being cut up in little pieces to sell off."

He followed her onto the elevator, dragging his feet. "And you're going to stop it?"

She stabbed the elevator button. "*We're* going to stop it, if we get there in time."

CHAPTER FOURTEEN

FROM THE HUMVEE, Carlotta called the garage, but only got the after-hours message.

"What are we going to do when we get there?" Wes asked, pushing the speed limit. Despite his grumbling, he was enjoying the adventure.

"I'll think of something," she said, pushing down the panic. In her mind's eyes, all she could picture was her beloved car hacked into pieces and sold off to the highest bidder like black market body parts.

Situated on a dead end street across from a row of storage units, the garage was an old brick building with three bays of glass and metal doors. When they pulled up, the windows were dark and the parking lot was empty except for a tow truck.

"Looks deserted," Wes offered.

"Stay here," she said, opening the door to jump down. She walked up to the bay of doors and peered in each one. The last door revealed a sight that made her stomach drop. Her Miata, tireless and sitting on cinder blocks, stripped of doors and fenders, looking naked and forlorn.

"Oh, no," she moaned.

"Did you find it?"

She jumped. She hadn't heard Wes come up behind her. "See for yourself."

He looked in the window and whistled low. "I always thought it was a sissy car, but still, that's sad."

"I have to get in there."

He turned his head. "That's crazy, Sis—what are you going to do? It's not as if you can drive it out of there."

The fact that he'd called her Sis cheered her only momentarily. "Will you help me?"

"Sure," he said without hesitation. "Tell me what to do."

The utter trust in his voice made her heart squeeze. She backed up and surveyed the front of the building. "Assuming there's a burglar alarm, we can't break open the office door, or breach the locks on the bay doors."

"No," Wes agreed. "But if we could remove the glass from one of these garage panels, you could probably wiggle your skinny ass through there."

She brightened. "You're right." She glanced down at her behind. "And thanks."

He took off his jacket, wrapped it around his fist, then punched the glass. On the second whack, it shattered. They froze, poised to run if an alarm sounded, but all was quiet. Wes used the jacket to clear the glass around the frame that was about eighteen inches by twelve inches.

"It's going to be a tight fit," she said, eyeing the opening. She shrugged out of the jacket and handed it to Wes. "Look…. if something weird happens, I want you to know I'm okay."

He squinted. "O… kay."

She gave him an impulsive kiss. "Just remember this conversation, and promise me you'll do something amazing with your life."

"You're freaking me out a little," he said nervously.

"I'll be back in a few minutes," she promised. "If I seem confused, just take me home, okay?"

He scratched his head. "O… kay."

She crouched down and stuck her head through the opening, then thrust in her arms and twisted her shoulders to work her way inside. The interior was cool and musty, reeking of motor oil and gasoline. She grimaced as she walked her hands through grime on the floor to pull herself through. After much grunting, she stood in the interior of the garage and wiped her hands on her pants. She went directly to her beloved car, her stomach twisting in anguish over its dissection. The shell that remained looked naked and violated. Without doors, she could climb directly into the driver's seat, which she assumed would be dismantled next.

She slid into the seat, mourning the car's state, wondering if it could be reassembled or if, like Humpty Dumpty, it couldn't be put back together again.

She put her hands on the steering wheel and closed her eyes, willing herself to be pulled across time, back to the place she'd come from. She channeled her thoughts and energy into her impending trip, imagining herself hurtling through space and landing in the townhouse garage.

After a few moments of silence, she opened her eyes... only to find herself still sitting in the dark body shop, her hands on the wheel of the disassembled Miata. Had the car's magic been dismantled along with its body parts?

Desperation welled up in her chest—now what? She slammed her hand on the steering wheel. In the ensuing white-hot explosion of pain in her head, she registered distantly that the airbag had deployed. She heard Wesley's voice calling to her before she blacked out...

CHAPTER FIFTEEN

"CARLOTTA? HEY...SIS...open your eyes."

Carlotta started awake to Wes's voice, her head pounding. She was disoriented, her gaze darting around the dark auto body garage.

No, not the auto body garage... the garage attached to the townhouse. And the Miata was still in one piece, with a cinnamon-orange air freshener dangling from the rear view mirror.

She was home.

"Earth to Carlotta."

She turned her head to see Wes's concerned face below bedhead hair. He stabbed at his glasses. "Are you okay?"

"I think so." But her voice sounded groggy even to her own ears.

"What the heck are you doing out here?"

"I... woke up early. I took a pain pill and came out here... I guess I fell asleep." She moved and grimaced.

"You're bleeding," he said, his face grim as he nodded to the red stain on her white shirt.

She looked down. "No, that's just strawberry preserves... from the bagel Mom toasted for me."

"Right," he said dryly, helping her from the car. "Delusional, much? Let's get you inside."

She allowed him to shoulder most of her weight as they headed across the front yard to the door. Dawn was breaking.

"I woke up and made breakfast and couldn't find you anywhere," he scolded. "You scared me to death."

"I'm sorry," she murmured. "I took a trip."

He eyed her warily. "How many pain pills did you take?"

"I… don't know," she admitted.

"Well, enough sleep for you. Let's get some food in your stomach. And check your shoulder dressing."

She let him talk, relieved to lean into him and happy to be back to life as she knew it. He helped her into the house and walked her through the living room into the kitchen where he deposited her in a chair. The aroma of eggs and bacon elicited a howl from her stomach.

"Let me take a look at your shoulder," he said, then eased down the collar of her shirt. His expression was serious. "It was bleeding, but it's dried now." He looked relieved.

"I didn't mean to worry you," she said, her heart brimming with love for her little brother. If she hated her parents for abandoning him, she loved that they were close because of it.

"It's okay." He straightened and moved to the stove, then carried over a skillet to fill the plates on the table. "It's a big day," he said cheerfully. "Dad is back. Are you up to visiting him?"

Her head was still pounding. She picked up her fork carefully. "I'm not sure."

"We can talk about it later," he said agreeably. "It's not as if he's going anywhere this time."

"True," she said.

Wes sat down and shook a napkin over his lap. "Sis, have you ever wondered… never mind." He shoveled in a mouthful of eggs.

She looked up. "What?"

He shrugged. "Have you ever wondered what our lives would've been like if Mom and Dad hadn't taken off?"

She nodded, and smiled. "Yes."

"And what do you think?"

She wet her lips. "I think our lives would've been different, but not necessarily better. I think we've done pretty well for ourselves, don't you?"

He hesitated, as if he had to think about it, then nodded.

She watched him devour his food just like any teenaged boy. But her head still reeled over the day she'd experienced… seeing Valerie, and Randolph, and everyone else. She wanted to freeze it in her brain so the memories wouldn't fade away. For a dream, it had seemed so real…

Her shoulder pinged with pain and when she moved, something fell onto the floor.

Wesley leaned over, then held up the item that had fallen from her shirt pocket: the cigar she'd bought from June for Randolph's celebratory party. It was still in the cardboard tube, and still wrapped with a red bow, if a little worse for wear from her "trip" home.

"What's this?" Wesley asked.

She stared, her mouth dropping open as she realized the implication of the souvenir from the other place.

"Sis?" he prompted.

"Uh… it's a gift… for you."

He grinned. "For me?" He opened the tube and removed the cigar, sliding it under his nose for a whiff. "Smells great—thanks!"

"You're welcome," she murmured. "Like you said… it's a big day."

Wes stabbed at his glasses. "This sounds weird, but I feel like my life is starting all over again."

She sent up a silent prayer of thanks for granting her wish… and for bringing her home. "I know exactly what you mean."

-The End -

A LONG-WINDED NOTE FROM THE AUTHOR

Thank you so very much for taking the time to read my BODY MOVERS novella! If you've been following along with the BODY MOVERS series, you know there was a break in the series after book 6, on a cliffhanger. That was my publisher's doing—they dropped the series in 2009 because it wasn't selling as well as they wanted. (Publishers don't care about cliffhangers.) In order to stay employed with them, I had to change direction and write something they thought would sell better. (Sadly, I have to pay my mortgage.)

Fast forward to 2011, and I, along with other authors who were fed up with the gatekeepers of traditional publishing houses, updated and re-released on my own as ebooks 11 titles I'd gotten rights back to over the years, and was pleasantly surprised when readers bought them...a lot of them! My eyes were opened to the possibilities of continuing my career with no one telling me what kind of book I had to write, what kind of cover was going to be on my book (whether I liked it or not), when it would be released, in what formats, at what price, etc. I was so excited!

Unfortunately, I was also still under contract to deliver a few more books. So I put my head down and worked like a demon to get out from under those obligations as quickly as I could. Meanwhile, I pulled out a couple of manuscripts that my publishers had turned down and updated those books to get them out, too. I was basically trying to get as much of my own material out there as quickly as I could so I could be financially free of my publishers to continue series they had dropped. One of those series is my beloved BODY MOVERS series.

I asked my publisher to sell me back the rights to the BODY MOVERS books; meanwhile, interest in the series had snowballed and readers were clamoring for the next book in the series. I knew I didn't have time to write a full-length book 7, so I came up with 6 ½ BODY PARTS to help bridge the gap between full length book 6 and full-length book 7. I hope you enjoyed it...I loved writing it! And I thought it was a much-needed exhale after the tension that built over books 4, 5, and 6.

And I'm happy to report that my publisher and I reached a compromise: they will continue to sell the ebooks, but I now have control of the print rights, so the books will be available in print again late summer 2013.

So...WHERE is book 7, you ask? I plan to release 7 BRIDES FOR 7 BODIES towards the end of 2013. I promise I WILL continue the BODY MOVERS series. How far out? I already have book 8 outlined...and I'll keep writing as long as you keep reading!

I apologize for that long-winded explanation, but my readers have been so patient with me, waiting for new books, I wanted you to know what was going on behind the scenes. The book industry is a frustrating business!

If you enjoyed 6 ½ BODY PARTS and feel inclined to leave a review on your favorite online bookstore, I would appreciate it very much. It will help to keep interest in the series alive.

And are you signed up to receive notices of my future book releases? If not, please drop by www.stephaniebond.com and sign up for my mailing list. I promise not to flood you with emails and I will never share or sell your address. And you can unsubscribe at any time.

Thanks again for your time and interest, and for telling your friends about my books. If you'd like to know more about some of my other books, please see the next section.

Happy reading!
Stephanie Bond

OTHER WORKS BY STEPHANIE BOND

Stories in the BODY MOVERS series:

PARTY CRASHERS (full-length prequel)
BODY MOVERS
2 BODIES FOR THE PRICE OF 1
3 MEN AND A BODY
4 BODIES AND A FUNERAL
5 BODIES TO DIE FOR
6 KILLER BODIES
6 ½ BODY PARTS (novella)
7 BRIDES FOR SEVEN BODIES coming in 2013

Humorous romantic mysteries:

TWO GUYS DETECTIVE AGENCY—*Even Victoria can't keep a secret from us...*
OUR HUSBAND—*Hell hath no fury like three women scorned!*
KILL THE COMPETITION—*There's only one sure way to the top.*
I THINK I LOVE YOU—*Sisters share everything in their closets...including the skeletons.*
GOT YOUR NUMBER—*You can run, but your past will eventually catch up with you.*
WHOLE LOTTA TROUBLE—*They didn't plan on getting caught...*
IN DEEP VOODOO—*A woman stabs a voodoo doll of her ex, and then he's found murdered!*
VOODOO OR DIE—*Another voodoo doll, another untimely demise...*
BUMP IN THE NIGHT—*a short mystery*

Romances:

ALMOST A FAMILY—*Fate gave them a second chance at love...*
LICENSE TO THRILL—*She's between a rock and a hard body...*
STOP THE WEDDING!—*If anyone objects to this wedding, speak now...*
THREE WISHES—*Be careful what you wish for!*
THE ARRANGEMENT—*Friends become lovers...what could possibly go wrong?*

Nonfiction:

GET A LIFE! 8 STEPS TO CREATE YOUR OWN LIFE LIST—*a short how-to for mapping out your personal life list!*

ABOUT THE AUTHOR

Stephanie Bond was five years deep into a corporate career in computer programming and pursuing an MBA at night when an instructor remarked she had a flair for writing and suggested she submit material to academic journals. But Stephanie was more interested in writing fiction—more specifically, romance and mystery novels. After writing in her spare time for two years, she sold her first manuscript, a romantic comedy, to Harlequin Books. After selling ten additional projects to two publishers, she left her corporate job to write fiction full-time. To-date, Stephanie has more than sixty published novels to her name, including the popular BODY MOVERS humorous mystery series. Look for the TWO GUYS DETECTIVE AGENCY series beginning in 2013. For more information on all of her books, visit www.stephaniebond.com.

Made in the USA
Lexington, KY
23 September 2013